Hits Keep Coming

Hits Keep Coming

K. McCoy

Published by be a muse productions, LLC, 2025.

HITS KEEP COMING

First edition. June 30, 2025.

ISBN: 979-8991737661

Written by K. McCoy.

Table of Contents

To the twelve-year-old me.

Thanks for keeping us safe, and know that you are loved.

"Yeah, it sholl is nice when what you have to say is well received. But life don't work like that baby girl. Putting yourself out there in this big ole world to get hurt is part of the life experience."

Hits Keep Coming
Written by K. McCoy

Trigger Warning

Please turn to the back of the book to see a list of detailed triggers before reading.

Prologue
The Summer of '95

One afternoon, with her Walkman blasting the latest track from Jade's favorite radio station, she saw a group of boys following her. Seeing one of her cousins with them, Jade chose to pretend not to see them. Until her cousin started to shout at her. Turning around to yell back, Jade's eyes grew twice their regular size when a rock darted toward her face.

"What y'all do that for?!" Jade shrieked while jumping to the side.

The boys laughed as they picked up more rocks. Jade's heart slammed hard into her chest before she took off running down the street.

"Dang! Her fat ass can run!"

Jade didn't turn around to see who was talking, her only goal was to get back home. But the boys started to run behind her too, and they were faster. Her eyes burned as she bolted around the corner. When Jade saw the silver buick in the yard, she wanted to shout from happiness.

Granny Gladys stood on the driver's side of the car, with a cigarette in one hand and the other on her hip. Jade didn't care that granny didn't keep her promise to stop smoking, all that raced through her mind was getting into the older woman's arms.

"What y'all chirrin doing now?"

Jade's whole chest was on fire, but she didn't dare stop. Reaching out her arms, she grabbed a hold of granny's small waist and wept when her granny's familiar scent made it to her nose.

"We was just playing!"

Hearing her older cousin lie, Jade looked up at her granny and the woman wiped Jade's eyes with her hand.

"That true Jade? Y'all was playing?"

4

When Jade shook her head, she saw her granny's eyes get smaller before looking out at the boys and flicking the cigarette into the air. "Y'all gone and play somewhere else, 'fore I start playing with a fresh switch!"

Soon Jade felt her granny's hands touch her back, causing more tears to stream down her round face.

"What happened baby girl?"

Jade sniffled. "I-I-I went to the store for more paper and w-when I was walking back home they th-threw rocks at me."

Her eyes stayed blurry, no matter how much she wiped at them with the back of her hands.

"You ain't say nothing to them?"

Looking up at granny Gladys, a fresh wave of hurt filled Jade's eyes. "I ain't say nothing to them!"

Then she did something that she knew could land a switch on her tail, but Jade didn't care, Jade pointed out to the road where the boys were and shouted, "They always picking on me! Why?!"

She could feel granny Gladys hands tighten against her shoulders, and Jade straighten her back. A child not 'staying in their place' and yelling at an adult was bad manners, so Jade knew that shouting at her granny was for sure going to end with her getting a sharp tree twig to her soft behind. She took a few more sharp breaths when granny Gladys' callused hand pinched her chin. It seemed like forever passed while granny stared down at Jade.

"I know you's mad, but you best 'member who you talkin' to, little girl."

Hearing granny scold her instead of having Jade walk to the big tree in front of their house, a new feeling of hope filled Jade's chest. "Yes ma'am." Jade mumbled out. A beat passed before she added, "I'm sorry."

Silence followed as granny let go of Jade's chin. "Well, they gone now. Anyway, I got something for you."

Trying to get her heart to slow down, Jade nodded and went with her granny to the passenger side of the four-door Buick. When the car door opened, a long black bag was in the first seat. At least it looked like a bag to Jade. "What is it granny?"

"You tell me. Gone and pick it up."

Jade put her bag of notes on one side as she reached out for the strange bag. It felt rough at first, but when Jade lifted it, she realized that there was something solid inside. Curious, she tilted her head and saw a zipper on the end. Turning back to her granny, she pulled on the zipper and saw what looked like shiny wood. Frozen in place, Jade was almost too scared to hope it was what she thought it was.

"I gotta gone back to work soon girl! Gone and take it out already. I know you know what it is by now."

Grinning wide enough to split her cheeks, Jade snatched the guitar out of the black bag. She'd wanted a guitar of her own after listening to the weekly top 40 for almost a year with granny and her auntie Dee. To know that she had one now made her feel so happy that she couldn't hold it in. Dropping the guitar back on the seat, Jade ran into granny's arms for a second time. "Thank you granny!"

"Well, don't thank just me. Dee gave me half the money to buy it. And there's some books inside one of them pockets too."

Looking back at the black bag, Jade finally saw the opening and the small books it held. She blinked away the new tears and whispered, "I'mma thank her too."

"It's our birthday present to you. So take good care of it, ya hear?"

Jade brought her lips together as her nose started to sting.

No one had gotten her a birthday present before. Growing up in a house with six other kids, she always heard the grown ups say how money was too tight for gifts on everyone's birthday. So Jade learned early to not ask for anything. To finally get something from her two favorite people in the world on her special day made Jade's heart grow in size.

She brought her eyes up to meet granny's one last time, "Thank you so much granny."

Granny Gladys bent down and kissed Jade's forehead. "You welcome."

Collecting the new notebooks and guitar, Jade looked at her granny and then across the street where her cousin and his friends were doing flips on an old mattress outside an abandoned house.

"You don't pay them no nevermind baby girl."

Clutching her gift, Jade hung her head. "Why ain't I like everybody else, granny?"

Feeling her granny's hands pull her chin up, Jade looked into her eyes. Granny didn't look mad. She looked like how Jade's friends sometimes did when they were trying to solve a hard math problem in class.

"You always been a little different. Nothing wrong with that – that's just who you are. Don't go trying to change to fit nobodies' mold of what *they* think *you* ought to be. That's how gems break baby – by giving in to pressures that weigh them down. You meant to shine. So you just keep on shining baby girl."

Jade liked when people remembered where the meaning of her name came from. And besides the not smoking no more part, she couldn't think of a time her granny ever not told her the truth. So Jade tried to stand up taller and nodded.

"Okay. I'mma try."

She picked up her bags with one hand and sprinted toward the house, turning one last time to wave at granny Gladys.

"I love you granny!"

Granny Gladys made her way to the driver's side of the Buick, but turned to face Jade. Sending a small smile back to her, granny got in the car and started the engine. And Jade stood in the doorway and watched her granny drive away, until the car was too far down the street to see anymore before going inside to finally play with her new gift.

October 2001

Chapter One
Sweet Valley Lows

Home was finally bearable, with everyone too busy to tease her anymore. She did have some school friends, but once that final bell rang, they all would go their separate ways. Every Friday, it was the same, she would walk with them until they reached the student car lot and when asked if she needed a ride, Jade would say no. Making her way to the city bus stop, she wondered, *Is this how it's gonna be for me now? When school ends?*

She tried to remember what granny Gladys told her years ago about accepting being different, but it was hard. Without granny here to remind Jade anymore, she felt so alone. Lung cancer took granny to the grave just before her 16th birthday, and since the day Jade had to watch the pallbearers carry her granny in the white and chrome casket to what was now her final resting spot, she felt alone.

Stepping off the city bus, Jade made her way through the tall gate entrance to Northern Lights High School. She didn't have any morning classes, but loved leaving the house as early as she could. With Luxe strapped to her back, Jade made her way to the music rooms that were just behind the administrative offices and squinted to see if any of the lights were on. Seeing a light further down the corridor, Jade made her way to the room. Until she heard someone call her name.

"You Jade, right?"

Jade surveyed the girl in front of her, and immediately recognized her. It was hard not to, since the short girl's photo was plastered all over campus. Kim was one of the popular kids always up for some award, played basketball and was now part of the orchestra, thanks to her saxophone playing boyfriend, another popular kid. "Hey. Yeah, my name's Jade."

"I thought so. I be seening you around here by yourself." the girl replied.

Jade really wanted to be alone and not take part in a social experiment, so she asked, "Is there another room open? I want to practice before classes start."

"Dang girl, you don't know how to talk to people?" Kim scoffed and said under her breath, "Guess that's why you ain't got no friends."

As Jade turned to leave, Kim spoke again. "I'm sorry, I ain't mean nothing by it. You can come sit with me. You know, before class starts"

Sighing, Jade forced a small smile on her face. "I'm straight. See you."

Not waiting for Kim to say another word, Jade turned on her heels and darted out of the music room. *I'm so done with these social experiments.*

Sometimes other girls, outside of Jade's small group of music friends, would come up and talk to her. In the early mornings before school, when Jade was in the library, after school, or pretty much whenever their 'real' friends weren't around. It started happening so much that Jade started to call the moments 'social experiments'.

These popular girls would tell Jade how they felt about everything - their fears about not fitting in, not really liking the boyfriends they had, or how scared they were about life after high school.

At first, Jade liked it. She liked the attention, and having someone to talk with about what life was gonna be like after high school. Especially after granny's death, the conversations made her feel less alone. Though the second when someone the girls knew would show up, they would forget that they were talking to Jade and leave without even saying goodbye.

But Jade remembered all of it.

Especially the look in the girls eyes when they would get up to leave with the ones they called friends. *They looked so sad. Like they had no choice but to go, even though they ain't want to.*

After her sophomore year of 'social experiments', Jade stopped feeling good about talking to those girls. And several months into her junior year, Jade was convinced that everything about high school was a waste of time.

But she did have one thing that she wanted. Jade wanted to study music after graduation. Last week at the school's college fair she listened to someone from Miami University talk about the music programs they offered, and when they gave her a postcard that showed off their conservatory, she wanted to know more. Which is why she scheduled a meeting with her assigned guidance counselor, Mr. Eagle.

Though after trekking across campus during free period and having to wait twenty minutes after her appointment time, Jade found herself sitting inside the small reception area wishing she'd just left school early to start looking for a part-time job.

The girl behind the big desk called her name and Jade turned to see a short lanky man wiping his face with a dark handkerchief.

"Mr. Eagle's ready to see you." was all the girl said before picking up the phone ringing at the desk.

Jade stood and walked through the warm office.

"S-sorry about the air conditioning." he offered, dapping at the corners of his eyes again. "Maintenance still hasn't made it out yet to fix the unit."

Jade didn't wait to be offered a seat as she plopped down in the chair. Mr. Eagle kept the door to his office open as he made his way to the desk. Shuffling a small brown folder while staring, he spoke again. "So, I believe you wanted to see me about potentially going to college?"

"Yeah."

He eyed the papers again and let out a chuckle, "Well, that's...that's a good goal to have."

The heat inside the tiny office, along with the voices outside and clanking of fingers on a keyboard stole the little focus Jade had left. She tried to focus and answer the man's questions, but everything around her was loud and draining her attention away. She managed to get through the general questions at least, until the older man asked how things were going at home.

That was when a group of basketball players rushed inside, laughing and stomping down the narrow corridor, their voices echoing loudly off the walls. With no more patience left, Jade snapped, "What my home situation got to do with anything?"

Staring at the many framed certificates and awards behind him that were hung on the wall, Jade waited for him to speak.

Mr. Eagle craned his head around to the window behind his desk and cleared his throat. "I see. Well, umm...are you involved in after-school activities?"

"No."

As the word left her mouth, Jade could feel her last chance at going to the University of Miami slip away. Jade knew it was a long shot, but she was getting desperate. And with her 18th birthday just a few months away, Jade knew it was only a matter of time before the woman trying to fill in as her guardian would start charging her rent. She had to know if she even had a chance at getting into Miami University. It was the only college she wanted to apply for - the only college she could afford to apply for, since they all came with admission fees. Jade had only managed to make enough playing on Luxe, her guitar, downtown for drunks to pay for one admission application.

If I have even a small chance of getting in, I have to know.

"Overall, you haven't been under any disciplinary action while at Northern Lights. And you speak well enough, with surprisingly good grades to boot!" Another chuckle, this time a little more shaky than the first one, slipped from his lips before he went on, "Though there is more that would be required before submitting an admission to college. Adding some extracurricular activities would really make your admissions stand out."

Jade stared at the older man, trying to make sure she heard him right. "If my grades are good enough, and I've already chosen my major- why I gotta do more?"

Seeing the fragile man look down while shuffling the paperwork in front of him, Jade waited as he quickly sighed. "Well, yes, you meet all the minimum requirements, that's true. However, colleges receive thousands of applicants each semester. And in order to improve your chances of being selected, you have to stand out. Being more involved in school clubs and organizations can help."

"Okay. Thanks." was all Jade could think to say. Not waiting to be asked, she stood up and made her way out of the office.

"I-I hope we can talk again soon, Ms. Thompson."

Rolling her eyes, Jade closed the door behind her. *Why I gotta be 'more involved' in high school stuff to go to college? That don't make no sense.*

Spotting the city bus at the traffic light just a block away from the school, Jade gripped her messenger bag and the black gig bag carrying Luxe tight before sprinting to the bus stop.

Chapter Two

The New Boy in Town

A week later Jade went with her sister Diamond to the Palms mall.

While Diamond was getting a mani and pedi at a nearby nail shop, Jade stopped inside the music store, SoundTracks. One of the few places that she could spend hours in, besides the library.

I really need this escape today!

There was a 'Help Wanted' sign hanging at the first register, prompting Jade to pause. Seeing a pen and a few blank application forms out front, she took one and began filling it out. Next to it was a white bin that said 'Completed Applications Here', so after finishing the form, Jade placed it into the bin as instructed. With that done, she made way to the international music aisle.

Since last year, more music from Japan and Korea had been added to the section, and Jade couldn't wait to hear the latest sounds. Reaching out to grab a CD from the boy group Bangers, Jade's hands came in contact with someone else's. Jumping backwards, she looked up with wide eyes to see a boy staring at her.

"Sorry, didn't see you."

He was the same height as Jade, with deep reddish brown skin and curly dark hair that had frosted white tips on the ends. Taking two steps back, Jade's lips parted to speak, but the boy in front of her beat her to it. "So, you a Bangers fan, uh? Name three of their top tracks then."

I know he ain't serious!

It was bad enough she had to let go of her dream college last week, but now having this dude test her like he had all the answers left Jade ready to fight. Narrowing her eyes, Jade finally spoke. "I'll do one better and name three reasons why you ain't shit."

When he didn't move, Jade put a hand on her hip and looked down at his appearance, scanning for anything to diss him with. "Your frost

14

tip dye job is pathetic and I can't decide what's dirtier - your denim jeans or them played out kicks."

"Two." the boy replied.

Seeing the guy in front of her smiling, Jade blinked."What?"

He walked up to Jade and placed a CD back onto the display case. "You said you'd name three reasons why I ain't shit, but I only heard two."

What's this fool's deal?

"I've been helping my Pops all day at his construction job, and I ain't had a chance to go back home and change. Though right now I'm kinda glad I didn't."

Jade froze.

No one ever responded to her insults like that before and it left her lost as to what to say next. Though the guy in front of her had more to say. "Name's Nashone."

"Jade! Let's go!"

She had never been so glad to hear Diamond yell for her in her whole life. Backing away slowly until she was several feet away from Nashone, Jade left SoundTracks.

"Who was that?" Diamond asked, admiring her French tip manicure.

"Who was who?"

Diamond cocked her head over to Jade as they walked outside of the mall and to her red Toyota Camry. "Your little friend. I saw him talking to you."

Rolling her eyes, Jade sighed. "I don't know him. I just went in and filled out an application."

"Uh, huh, if you say so. He was kinda cute. You should've gave him the house number."

She knew Diamond was joking, but just the thought of anyone calling her - especially a boy - at the house made Jade queasy. To shake off the feeling, Jade flippantly replied, "Nah! Enough boys call the house anyway, thanks to you."

Scratching the back of her head, Jade listened as Diamond started the engine and sucked her teeth. "I was just trying to give you some free advice. You wouldn't have to worry about getting no job if you was like me."

Jade sighed while putting on her seat belt. Feeling claws scratch the left side of her head in between where her thick cornrows and mini fro met, Jade yelped.

"And this natural look ain't doing you no favors either! Need to gone 'head and let me take a straight comb to that mess." Diamond tsked before pulling out of the parking lot.

Thinking back to the boy she just met, how he wasn't fazed by anything she said, Jade couldn't think of anything clever to say to Diamond's comment about her hair. Which must be why her sister kept talking, "I'm just saying. Maybe if you relax your mane and your mouth more, folks will relax around you too. You'd finally have something to do on the weekends instead of avoiding mama and strumming that dang guitar. Withcho rude 'lil ass."

"I love you, Diamond, but I ain't going back to the creamy crack."

Diamond reached out her hand and Jade instinctively tilted her head toward the window while her older sister turned on the radio, causing Diamond to laugh. "Just wait - one of these nights when you sleeping, I'mma creep in your room and lather you right on up!"

Images of waking up to Diamond looming over her wearing gloves and holding an African Pride box in the middle of the night left Jade's overactive brain going into high gear.

Knowing her crazy ass, she just might try that mess. Let me start sleeping with an extra satin scarf from now on.

The two heard one of their favorite songs and began rapping along, giggling as Diamond weaved through the midday traffic.

***

That next Monday, Jade and a few friends walked into their strings class together. Until Lucky, another guitarist, stopped mid-sentence. Jade almost cussed, since she was walking directly behind her classmate and abruptly stopped, causing a few others to roughly bump against her back where Luxe was strapped.

"Dang! Who's *he*?"

Jade's attention went to where Lucky stared off to, and she wanted to immediately walk out of the room.

Why's he here?

While the others murmured about the new boy in their third period class, Jade was doing her best to make sure he didn't notice her. Stepping back, she let her friends walk in front and took a seat as close to the classroom door as possible. Hearing the morning bell, the other students sat as well, and they continued talking until their teacher entered. Making their way to the front of the class, the man stopped when the new guy stood up and handed him a form. Looking over it, their teacher nodded and turned to face the class. "Everyone, say hello to Nas-on Micheals."

"It's Na-shone. Nashone Daniels, sir."

A few students giggled as their teacher nodded while scribbling in their black and red school planner. "You all make sure to help Nashone here get settled in, okay?"

Not waiting for a response, their teacher went to their desk and picked up the attendance folder to take roll.

Dang! I forgot 'bout roll call.

Trying not to panic, Jade slowly eased out of her seat and grabbed Luxe along with her school bag. Just as she was a few feet away from reaching the door handle to freedom, their teacher called out, "In a hurry to leave already, Ms. Jade?"

The snickers that followed wouldn't normally bother Jade, but knowing that she'd been spotted left her with no choice than to face the front of the class. "I, uh, I remembered I had to see the front office about something." she weakly mumbled.

"Whatever it is, it can wait until after class. Sit back down, please."

Jade did as she was told and tried to ignore the stares as she went back to her seat. Class resumed and Jade could feel Nashone staring at her. While looking over her completed theory exercises, she finally got up the nerve to look ahead. Sure enough, the boy from the record store last weekend was staring directly at her.

Showing off all his teeth, Nashone raised a hand her way, to which Jade inhaled sharply before grabbing her workbook. Pulling it up high enough to cover her face, Jade heard a snort and quickly lowered the book to find Nashone turning back around in his seat and shaking his head.

Girl focus! Finish your work so you can bounce before the bell rings.

Closing her eyes, Jade pried one open and sighed in relief when she found Nashone's back facing the class. She then put her workbook back down and went to work on the day's lesson as fast as possible. Completing the last exercise, Jade tore the worksheet from her book and went to turn it in to her teacher.

"Can I go to the front office now?"

When her teacher nodded, Jade grinned.

Walking back to her desk to collect her things, she almost didn't hear when their teacher called her name.

"Please accompany our newest student to the front office, since you're heading there too. He needs to turn in his paperwork to the administrative desk."

Several girls in the class raised their hands before one blurted out, "I can take him!"

Their teacher narrowed his eyes at the girl that spoke before raising his voice to ask, "Are you finished with today's assignment?"

When the other student said nothing, their teacher continued, "Thank you for the offer, but I'm certain that Jade can take Nashone there just fine."

I don't wanna take him anywhere! This ain't fair!

The other girls put their hands down and darted their eyes between Jade and Nashone. Jade watched as Nashone stood up and made his way to her. He was dressed in a clean black FUBU t-shirt and pair of fresh denim jeans that sagged, almost covering his all white sneakers. As he walked next to her, Jade heard the gold chains that Nashone wore around his neck chime low, stopping when he stood next to her. Jade quickly looked away when she saw his head turn her way.

"You two are dismissed."

Jade's head was as she stomped back to her desk to grab her things, making sure to strap Luxe tightly while walking out of the classroom. The hallway was quiet when they stepped out, and Jade tried to be thankful for the silence. Until Nashone started to fill it by speaking.

"So, you really was gonna act like you ain't see me?"

Just ignore him.

She picked up her pace, leaving Nashone a few feet behind before he quickly caught up.

"Hey, slow down!" he started before asking, "Why you rushing?"

Turning the corner down the brick hall, Jade stopped and pointed. "The admin office is through there. I'm out."

When she started to go in the other direction, Nashone reached out and grabbed her wrist. Jerking her hand away, she almost lost her balance before remembering where Luxe was and quickly righting herself.

"But didn't you tell the teacher you had to... oh."

Watching Nashone piece together what she didn't say, Jade thought she was good to go. She gave him one last glance from behind before walking away and found him staring.

Why ain't he going to the dang office?

Before Jade could ask him herself, the bell rang, followed by the sounds of doors opening and students rushing out of their classrooms. She kept looking at Nashone until he finally walked toward the admin building, leaving Jade standing in the hallway as the other students passed by to get to their next class.

Jade didn't see Nashone again until the end of the day. When she did, he was surrounded by a group of students outside near the student pick up area. Slipping on a pair of headphones and pressing play on her new mp3 player, Jade walked past the small crowd to get to the city bus, making sure to keep her eyes straight ahead.

***

Coming home to an empty house, Jade welcomed the silence. She thought Diamond would've been home before her, but didn't see Diamond's ride out front as she used the house key to let herself inside. Not seeing anyone Jade shrugged her shoulders and walked to her room.

Well, I better get dressed before she shows up to take me to work.

While taking off her shirt, Jade couldn't shake the feeling that someone was watching her.

She paused to look around her room and saw that the room door was cracked open. After closing it, Jade finished getting dressed. She heard a door open while putting on her work shoes and prayed it was Diamond.

Let me go meet her at the front door, so I ain't gotta see that woman today.

The minute the woman with her face found out Jade had a job, she demanded that Jade start paying rent - just like Jade knew she would.

Just the thought of paying that woman rent when she never worked a day in her life made Jade want to cuss.

Thanks to granny Gladys, she ain't had never had to work to pay the house note.

Jade knew she'd rather be homeless than hand her so-called guardian money. Marching down the hallway back to the front door, Jade almost jumped out of her skin at the sight of a shirtless man sitting in the living room with his legs spread open. His denim jeans were covered in different stains and eyes were glued on her.

"Don't worry baby, ion bite." he drawled out with one of his hands inching up his thigh and the other stroking his gray beard. When the older man flashed Jade a full mouth of gold teeth her brain shrieked.

It'd been awhile since she had seen a 7-2-7. That's what Jade called the men her guardian would bring to the house from seven o'clock at night to seven in the morning. And from the smell that clung to her nose the longer she stood in his presence, this one hadn't bothered using the shower since being there.

"Who the hell are you?" she barked.

He chuckled low. "Oh, you got a little bite to ya, uh? Bet I can straighten yo young ass right on out..."

The way he stared at her made Jade's skin crawl. But before Jade could get in another word, she heard footsteps behind. "Why you out here while I was sleeping baby?"

Jade rolled her eyes as she turned to face the woman, who narrowed her eyes. "Ain't you got a job? Why you here during the day?"

Taking in her so-called guardian's disheveled clothes, the smell of liquor, and stale cigarettes, Jade guessed they had been up and at it all night.

I can't wait to get out of here.

Jade ignored their stares as she gripped the straps to her gig bag and walked to the front door.

***

She thought she'd hate working, but so far, Jade really liked being a part-time team member at SoundTracks. Especially during the night shift. Hardly any customers came in during that time on the weekdays.

And she got to choose what music played in the store after eight o'clock.

So lost in the latest mellow yet upbeat jazz track that flowed from the music system, Jade wasn't paying much attention to where she was walking. She collided with a customer, bringing all the vinyl records in her hands to the ground.

"I'm so sorry! I wasn't..."

The sight of Nashone standing in front of her stopped Jade from speaking.

"So you *do* have basic social skills."

Jade closed her eyes before sighing and looking around the store. *Please don't let my manager come out of the office right now.*

"I'm working. Can you take your attitude somewhere else?" she hissed.

Nashone's eyes doubled in size, "*My* attitude? You the one that's been frontin' - actin' like you can't acknowledge my presence."

She bent down to pick up the records from the floor. Taking her time, Jade hoped that Nashone would get the hint and leave, but after picking up the last vinyl she noticed that he hadn't moved from the spot in front of her. Releasing a heavy sigh, Jade righted herself, clutching the vinyl records close.

"I see you, alright? Later."

Turning to walk away, Jade tried to calm down her rapidly beating heart. *He ain't all that no way. Probably just not used to being ignored, but he'll start avoiding me soon too.*

Once she was up to the display rack, Jade began to sort out the vinyl by artist and music genre.

"So you work here? That's cool." Nashone said from behind her.

I won't be working here long, if your bug-a-boo ass don't leave me alone!

"You must really like music to work here." He added.

Getting desperate to get rid of him once and for all, Jade forced herself to try and talk to him. With the last vinyl up on display, she braced herself for facing Nashone again. Only a few feet remained between them, and Jade couldn't help but send a small smile back his way. His grin was brighter than the fluorescent light in the store as Nashone leveled his eyes to hers.

"I-it's straight."

Jade heard a group of people laughing when entering the record store and her worry meter almost broke when she realized that they were all varsity players from school. Pinned between the display case and Nashone, Jade's throat went dry while her eyes went in search of a place to hide.

"How long you been working here? The last time I came here, you were listening to a stack of CDs."

No way am I gonna let them clown me in this big ass place!

She didn't care if she got fired - it had to be better than whatever they were planning to do. Jade watched the guys push each other around and point at the posters over in the Hip Hop section, before bringing her eyes to Nashone. And he really did look like he wanted to keep talking. Though Jade's instincts were all but shouting at her to leave. She really couldn't put into words why, but the feeling shot up from her gut to her chest, forcing her to finally move away from Nashone.

"Yeah. See you around." Jade tightly closed her eyes as her voice came out as a whisper.

Nashone stared at her for a second until they noticed a customer standing at the register. "You ain't gonna go back to ignoring me?"

Shaking her head, Jade scurried away to the opposite side of the store. She kept her eyes on the group, even while ringing up customers. Finally, the night manager came out from the back room and Jade looked on while they surveyed the store.

"Everything okay out here, Jade?" the manager asked.

When she nodded, they continued with the question she'd been waiting on since seeing the group of guys come in. "Well, since we only got an hour left and it's slow, you want to head out for the night?"

Jade wanted to shout out her reply, but instead nodded. "Yeah, I'd like to leave. Please."

"Sure thing. Just close down your register and call me when you're done."

She watched as the night manager strolled off and went to work on getting her register closed out. Caught up in making sure the numbers matched the sales from the day, Jade didn't hear one of the guys call her name.

"Yo! String geek - you don't hear me talking to you?"

The shorter guy of the group finally got Jade to look over at him. Pausing her counting, Jade placed her hand on the cool surface before testing out a new comeback, "Sorry, I couldn't see you from over the counter. "

Hearing a snort from in the crowd, Jade smiled softly. Until the shorter guy barked at her again, "You stay having jokes, withcho fat ass!"

"Aye - you ain't gotta talk to her like that."

Jade's eyes widened when she saw Nashone walk up to the shorter guy. He stood directly in front of the guy as the others looked on.

"You just got here newbie, so maybe you don't know. But this one ain't worth your time." Another guy said.

Nashone looked over his shoulder and scoffed, "Who I'm friends with is my business."

"What? You wanna be friends with this crazy chick?" the short guy asked in disbelief. "Everybody knows she ain't got no friends!"

Looking between the group and her, Nashone brought his attention back to Jade. "Guess that makes me your first."

This fool crazier *than me!*

Nashone grinned when he faced the others again, "Yeah, I think I do wanna be friends with the crazy chick."

"Whatever man." The short guy said as he marched over to the others. "Let's bounce y'all." The group followed him out the store, but not before one of them pushed over a rack of CDs near the entrance.

Jade quickly finished counting her register and took it to the back room to give to the manager. When she came back out, with Luxe on her back, Jade saw Nashone standing at the rack with the CDs in his hands.

"I thought you might want some help with these."

No one had been this helpful, or even kind, to Jade in a minute. Outside of her sister, and the few friends Jade made over the last year, at least. And there was also the way Nashone kept looking at her, like he was hoping for a pat on the head for a job well done. Jade didn't like it. Especially the fact that her hands itched to do just that whenever he smiled her way.

"Why?" Jade finally asked.

Nashone grinned at her again and Jade fought the urge to touch his cheeks. "It's a lot of CDs on this case, so-"

"No. Why are you being nice to me? What you want?"

"Why do I have to want something from you?"

Jade rolled her eyes, "That's how all these social experiments go. Y'all see me alone and come over and start talking like we're friends. Until someone cool shows up."

By the time Jade realized what she'd let slip out, Nashone had put the last CD back on the case and was walking toward her. He stared for a beat before saying, "What social experiment? And didn't you hear me from before? I said I wanna be your friend."

He did say that, but Jade's brain was struggling to make what Nashone said make sense.

"Look, I know you just met me. And from what those dudes said, I get why you feel the need to ask 'bout me."

Jade waited for him to continue, her eyes stayed on Nashone as he cleared his throat. "But like ole boy said, I'm new here. And I like you."

Her eyes widened and Nashone backed up a few feet, chuckling as he shook his head. "I mean, I like your style. You ain't scared to speak your mind or nothing. Like, that's cool as fuck to me."

Feeling her cheeks warm up, Jade lowered her head for a second before meeting Nashone's stare. He stood a little taller than before and Jade let a small smile slip through. "Okay."

"Okay?"

Jade glanced around the store before letting out a small laugh. "Okay, fine. I guess we can hang out."

"That's what's up! Then you can tell me what's a sista in the south doing listening to boy band groups from East Asia."

Jade smirked. "I'll tell you, soon as you tell me how you know they from Asia."

The two glanced at one another before breaking out into a fit of laughter.

***

After that night at the record store, Jade went to school and found Nashone already inside the music room. He greeted Jade with a smile that warmed her heart, along with her cheeks.

"I heard you come in here real early. And, umm, I wanna ask you to help me with somethin'..."

Jade closed her eyes as she stepped further into the room, removing Luxe from her back. When she turned around to take the guitar out of its bag, she took two short breaths and slowly opened her eyes again.

"W-what do you need my help with, exactly?"

Sitting down in the stool furthest away, Jade wanted to stand again when Nashone started to make his way closer. She made sure to keep her eyes locked on Luxe's strings.

"I'm still new to this whole music thing. And, umm..you seem to have been doing this for a while."

Nashone paused and met Jade's stare. Seconds passed and she waited for him to say more. He then took out his music theory book and held it up to his chest, sending a small grin Jade's way. When she laughed, Nashone's smile disappeared and Jade lowered her stare.

"You've never had to ask for help before, have you?"

Curious, Jade brought her eyes up to meet his. Nashone's hazel eyes seemed to glow as he bored into Jade's. Looking at him, she almost lost track of time.

The silence in the room seemed to be sucking her into his orbit, as Nashone took another step into Jade's personal space. His eyelashes fluttered in front of her, and Jade wanted to reach out a hand to feel if they were as soft as they appeared.

"Nah, not really."

When did his voice get so deep?

"Look, back at my old school, we ain't had all of this."

Nashone gestured with his hands around the room and the scent of something sweet yet spicy made its way to Jade's nose.

"I was in a choir there, but I didn't know all the stuff you do. Like musical compositions and metronomes and shit."

Jade chuckled as she watched Nashone look away and titled his head to the side. She thought about her first summer back in ninety-five, studying the basic theory in those books she got on her thirteenth birthday. The year after that, Jade started middle school and joined the guitar club. She was so scared to ask for help that she'd stay after school studying all the chord progressions and theory she could, until the janitor would show up and she'd have to leave.

But it was worth it. Especially now.

Remembering that the junior recital was coming up, Jade got an idea. Before she could lose her nerve, she cleared her throat and looked directly at Nashone. "Okay, I'll help you, but only on two conditions."

Nashone rolled his eyes. "Here you go. I should've known it wouldn't be easy..."

Jade fought the corners of her lips from turning upward as she continued. "First of all, ain't nothing worth having easy, so yeah, you gotta put in the work. Don't come asking for help and think your good looks and charm are gonna do all the heavy lifting."

"You think I look good?" Nashone asked.

She ignored his question, as the butterflies slowly fluttered around in her stomach. "We study and practice everyday before class. You got me?"

Nashone nodded.

"And you have to do this year's recital with me as your accompaniment."

Squinting his eyes, Nashone asked, "What's a recital?"

I know you lyin'! How he not *know what a recital is?!*

"When students get dressed up and showcase their musical talents to an audience. Mainly to the teachers and other music students. Kinda like performing at an open mic. That's a recital."

He backed away from Jade, shaking his head, "Oh hell nah! I ain't doing all that!"

"Well, you gotta. It's like a final score for all students in a music class." Jade explained. *And if you want my help, you for sure gonna do it. This way I still get recital credit as an accompanist.*

Keeping her face calm, Jade watched as Nashone looked at her and the door.

"You for real?" Nashone finally asked.

This time, Jade didn't bother with hiding the smile on her face. "As real as a heart attack."

He picked up his notebook and let out a sigh. "Alright. When do we start?"

"Right now."

Chapter Three
Gone

Jade stamped on her right foot as she waited for the city bus to pick her up. When it finally arrived, she pressed her monthly rider pass to the token machine and quickly sat down.

Dang! I hope Nashone ain't running late either.

A smile fought its way through as she thought about the last few weeks of studying and practicing with Nashone for their recital piece next month. They finally agreed on a song that was in Nashone's vocal range and that Jade could learn well enough to play with Luxe.

"Hey pretty baby - you wanna get off with me?"

The elderly man sitting behind Jade snapped her out of her thoughts when he loudly spoke. Whipping her head in his direction, Jade was surprised he could move, much less speak, since his business suit appeared to be at least two sizes too small. Her smile was gone in an instant when she turned her lips down from seeing his cocky grin.

"Whatayada say? Wanna slide out with me at the next stop?"

Turning to face the front of the bus, and started rummaging inside her bag. With the mp3 player in her hands, Jade placed her headphones into each ear and pressed play.

It was only a few minutes after six o'clock when Jade got to the school and she wasted no time getting to the music building. Just as she turned the corner, Jade saw the janitor turn on the hallway lights and her smile returned. She rushed to the second music practice room and swung open the door, almost dropping her messenger bag in the process. Placing it on the piano bench, Jade removed her gig bag straps and took out Luxe. Luckily she had tuned it last night before bed, so Jade sat on the stool and slowed down her breathing by taking a deep breath and warming up with a random fingering exercise.

"Life ain't all bad. Gotta enjoy the moments when they..."

That was my last entry in the notebook! Wh-

Jade's eyes widened as her head jerked up and she saw Nashone walking toward her. He was holding her green composition book and looking down at the pages. She almost dropped Luxe on the floor, gripping the neck of the guitar while hopping off of the stool.

"What's up? Did you miss me?" Nashone grinned seeing Jade coming toward him, but when she reached out for the book, he extended his hand in the air. "This yours?"

"Yes. Now give it to me." Jade answered sharply.

Nashone chuckled, "Say please."

The look Jade sent his way made Nashone back up a few feet. "Dang girl, I was just playing. Take your little book."

Jade snatched the book out of his hands and placed Luxe on top of the piano as she put it back into her messenger bag. When she closed the bag, Jade took a few more deep breaths before turning to face Nashone.

"Sorry, I ain't mean to make you all mad and shit. The book was on the floor when I got here last night, so I picked it up."

"Thank you. Let's go ahead and start." Jade finally said.

Instead, Nashone looked over at her guitar and then back to Jade. A soft smile flashed across his lips. "Ah, I get it now."

Squinting at him, Jade asked, "What?"

"You really into this music shit. Like, you wanna do this for real someday. Right?"

Jade said nothing as she took at the sheet music for their recital piece, keeping her eyes on the music stand.

"Why else you study so hard? Coming in before everybody else, working at the record store...You planning to do this when school's over, ain't you?"

Jade looked at Nashone and released a soft sigh. "I dunno. Maybe."

The room was quiet and that seemed to make Jade's chest tighten. Clearing her throat, she pointed to the sheet music in front of them and Nashone laughed.

***

It's finally recital week! Yes!

Jade couldn't remember being this excited to get to school. She briskly walked through the empty hallway, until getting to the music practice rooms. Turning on the lights, Jade removed Luxe from her shoulders and placed the bag on top of the piano. Nashone was always late, but today it didn't faze Jade as she gently took her guitar out of the gig bag and sat down in the nearest chair. Her right hand moved to the lowest string and Jade brought her thumb and index finger around it, softly pulling on it. Then she looked over at the keys on the piano and found the one that matched the note on Luxe.

Sounds slightly off, but that's cool. I got time.

A few minutes went by while Jade checked each string on Luxe to make sure that they all were the right sound. When she finished, Jade glanced up at the large clock near the door and frowned.

Where he at? Classes gonna start soon.

It was too early to call him, since the free minutes on her cell phone didn't start until after eight at night. But Jade took out her phone anyway. Sighing, she searched for Nashone's name in the recent messages and sent him a text instead, asking him where he was.

To keep her hands busy, Jade started to practice the plucking technique from her one on one lessons with the music department's guitar instructor. The tempo was where she'd always struggled, so Jade began slowly with the piece she was learning to memorize for her senior recital next year. Everything was going well, until Jade heard sneakers dragging and scuffing the ground outside her room. She was now moving at the normal, but quicker pace of the melody and darted her eyes to the door when the sharp pain reached Jade's hand.

Ouch! What the-

Looking down, Jade saw that the nylon D string had separated from the bridge of her acoustic guitar. The pain in her hand increased and she gasped from the sight of blood that appeared on her left hand.

I don't have time for this today!

Putting down Luxe, Jade eased the guitar back into its gig bag and put away her sheet music. She glanced up at the clock and sighed on her way out of the room. Since the first aid kits were only in the classrooms and the nurse's station, Jade carefully pulled one of the gig bag straps over her shoulder and gingerly held her throbbing left hand out before walking to the nurse's office.

While walking over to the nurse's office, she heard her phone ring but couldn't answer it. Putting more of a pep in her step, Jade made it to the office and saw more students arrive on campus. "Morning. Can I get a bandaid please?"

The nurse saw her and asked several questions while cleaning Jade's wound. She was convinced that the woman hardly saw anyone, as she insisted on wrapping Jade's hand properly with ointment, a wrap around gauze, and tape.

"Thank you." Jade mumbled on the way out.

Hearing the first bell, she trudged on to the library and waited for class to end. Since this was technically her free period, Jade went into one of the empty rooms to check her phone. The text from Nashone was short, just the words 'sorry' showed up on the screen.

Maybe he woke up late? I'm surprised he been showing up on time this much, to be honest.

With nothing else to do, Jade took out her notebook and read the passages she'd written in it earlier that week until the end of class bell rang.

Guess he'll tell me what happened before class.

Though when Jade walked into their theory class, Nashone wasn't there. The heavy feeling from before came back and she shook it off when Lucky sat next to her.

"What's up?" her friend asked, looking at Jade's bandaged hand.

Jade shrugged. "This? Nothing. Just one of the new steel strings I bought snapped this morning."

Lucky scoffed. "I tried to tell you that you tune your guitar too much!"

"Whatever." Jade said before asking, "You seen Nashone yet?"

"Un huh. I ain't seen him."

Their teacher walked into the room just as the final bell rang and Jade kept her eyes on him while quietly slipping out her blue Nokia phone. When the teacher started writing on the blackboard, Jade typed a quick text to Nashone, asking if everything was straight.

The feeling from earlier spread down from Jade's chest, to her stomach and had reached her other limbs once school ended and she hadn't heard back from Nashone. *Why ain't he text me back already?*

***

Another day passed, and no Nashone. Jade was finally able to call him the night before but he didn't answer. And the next day after school the same thing happened.

She even thought about mustering up the nerve to ask the popular kids at school if they'd heard from him, but the thought of them clowning her kept Jade from doing that. When her alarm went off on Friday, the morning of their scheduled recital, Jade felt her eyes sting as she got dressed and packed her recital bag. With tired yet trembling hands, she dialed Nashone's number one last time.

The number you called is no longer in service. Please try your call again.

Pressing end on her phone, Jade beat the sunrise as she walked to the city bus stop. The ride was quiet, since it was almost the weekend and less people caught the bus that early on Fridays. Jade felt knots form in her stomach with each designated stop the bus made. By the time the bus got to school, Jade was tempted to not pull on the stop cord, instead just stay on the bus until it drove across the bridge to the other side of town.

As her hands yanked on the cord, Jade's throat burned.

Why would Nashone do me like this? I thought- I thought he was really my friend.

The night he announced to everyone at SoundTrack replayed in Jade's mind, along with the days she spent helping him understand the basics to music theory more. Each laugh and smile from their time together flashed before her while Jade dragged her feet to the second music practice room. When she reached the door, her knees swayed when Jade touched the door knob. Once inside, she flipped off the room light and slumped to the floor. A hollow thump sound was heard when the gig bag she carried Luxe in joined her on the ground. Hot tears welled up and quickly left Jade's eyes as her head rested on the cold metal door.

With her eyes closed, Jade wiped at her face and sat in the silent room until the morning bell rang.

What I'm gonna do now?

Jade knew that she'd still have to perform, but after last year's recital where the seniors snicker out in the crowd at Jade for singing one of the songs she wrote to a simple three chord progression, she would rather clean the band room for the rest of the school year then go through that again.

Getting up from the floor, she blinked her eyes while they re-adjusted to the fluorescent lights. Putting the gig bag on top of the piano, Jade unzipped the front pocket and took out her Classic Guitarist songbook. Flipping through each page, she skimmed each one until she found a piece she felt okay about performing on short notice. There wasn't much time, but the more Jade stared at the sheet music, she knew she could perform it for the recital. Jade couldn't remember the last time she'd practiced any of the Classics in the book, but she did have an hour or so to practice.

I can do this - I have to do this.

Before she got started Jade left the practice room to go change into her recital attire in the nearest restroom.

"What's up Jade! You looking good"

Jade turned to see Lucky and some other girls walk into the restroom as she was leaving.

"Thanks."

Lucky walked up to her and whispered, "You doing the recital solo? No one has seen Nashone all week."

Blinking her eyes fast, Jade nodded and Lucky placed a hand on her shoulder. "Good Luck."

"Thanks."

While strapping the soft gig bag onto her back, Jade strolled out of the restroom. Turning the corner to head back to the practice room, Jade spotted Lucky again. This time Lucky was on the phone, speaking in Spanish. And when she ended the call, Jade thought Lucky would start crying as she took in her bloodshot eyes.

"Lucky, everything alright?" Jade asked.

Her friend looked up at her and her eyes were full of unshed tears when she shook her head. "My big brother just came out to my parents. Th-they told him he has to move out."

Jade took a step closer and whispered, "Dang, I'm sorry Lucky."

"I begged him not to tell them! But since he's already found a place to rent near his college campus, I guess he knew how it'd go down."

Wrapping an arm around Lucky, Jade waited for her friend to pull away. "I don't know your brother, but I know what he did couldn't been easy."

Seeing a small smile across Lucky's face, Jade returned it.

"My brother Xavier really is the bravest person I know, no doubt."

"I hope I can meet him someday." Jade said just as the next bell rang. "But first, I gotta get through this recital."

The two chuckled before going their separate ways.

***

Classes seem to pass by at warp speed, and before Jade had time to think, it was fourth period and she was walking to the main band room. Inside the room was the school's only grand baby piano and for today's recitals, the black chorus chairs were spaced out in a half circle. All three music teachers were there, front and center in the room behind a small square table with forms and notebooks, ready to check and write down their critiques for each performer.

Jade went to the third row of chairs and sat down at the end seat. She listened as one of the teachers called out a student's name and watched the fair skin girl walk forward to them and bowed slightly before stating which piece she would be performing solo. When the student sat down at the piano without any sheet music, Jade saw her chest rise and fall for a moment before she struck the first key. The student's hands floated across the white and black percussion titles, face twisted in the most serious display of concentration Jade had ever seen.

Damn, she's good.

Lost in watching and hearing the performance, Jade didn't notice the other students that had slipped in and sat down in the back of the room.

"Jade Thornton and Nashone Daniels."

Hearing his name after hers made Jade feel as if someone had wrapped steel strings around her heart and pulled, squeezing the strings tighter around her heart. "Jade Thornton and Nashone Daniels, please come to the front of the class."

Jade moved fast, unsheathing Luxe from the soft bag and smoothing out the bottom of her tucked in off white blouse as she made her way to the teachers. Two of them looked around before

Jade's music theory teacher spoke. "Since Daniels has been absent all week, is it safe to assume you will be performing a solo piece instead of providing an accompaniment?"

"Y-yes sir."

Clutching Luxe's neck tight enough to see the whites to her fingertips, Jade took a deep breath and exhaled slowly when she bowed slightly to the teachers. The female teacher on the far end of the table, with olive skin and salt and pepper hair slicked back in a coiffed haircut, looked Jade over and glanced behind her. "Very well. We will allow you a few minutes to change into your recital attire."

Jade tightly shut her eyes as a few students chuckled behind. "Ma'am, I'm wearing my recital attire."

The older woman turned to face the other teachers as Jade rushed out a question that she desperately needed answered.

"May I begin please?"

A beat passed until the older woman spoke again, "Proceed."

She almost sprinted to the stool opposite the teacher's table, placing Luxe on top. Jade's hand shook briefly when she put the Classic Guitarist songbook on the music stand, taking care to make sure it was flat against the stand and wouldn't move. Now that she wasn't facing anyone, just her music and Luxe, Jade could feel her heartbeat begin to return to normal.

You can do this. You have to do this.

Closing her eyes and focusing on her breathing, Jade began to read the sheet music and when the first chord count arrived, she brushed the strings and went to strum the guitar. Only her fingering is off and instead of strumming right away, Jade hit the last E string.

The chord was for an E sharp, better to give them a sound close to it than clunk out a whole wrong ass chord - keep going!

Inhaling sharply, Jade changed up the piece just once more and finger picked the quick tempo of the chords, instead of strumming them for the next two counts. Her throat is parched and the fear of what pitch may come out clawed its way to the inside of her mouth, sealing it shut. Jade continued with the piece, sticking as close to the original sheet music as possible.

Once the last chord she plucked played out, fading into the air, Jade gave the teachers her attention and bowed again before removing the book from the stand. Her music theory teacher offered a smile and Jade tried to return it before settling on another short bow, making sure to keep her hands to the sides.

Sitting down as far back from the other students, Jade tried to listen to the other performers, but her thoughts were back in the practice room. More memories of her last time there with Nashone popped up into her mind. And no matter how many times she tried to make them go away, the images kept coming.

"Thank you all. Your performances and assessments will be available for review next week. Until then, have a good day everyone!"

After the other male teacher spoke, Jade stood and left the classroom. She was so glad she agreed to pick up someone else's shift that night at SoundTracks, because Jade needed something to look forward to.

The bus ride back to her childhood home seemed to be quicker than it normally was. She found herself walking through the front door of the house, looking around for something - anything that would tell Jade to stay. But there was nothing.

I should have left when granny Gladys died.

Jade finally opened the door to her room and immediately crumbled into the twin size bed. She lifted up her shoulders, one at a time, and slipped her guitar bag down until it laid on the bed beside her.

Nashone's face appeared the minute Jade closed her eyes.

Girl, stop wondering what happened. Whatever it was, he couldn't be bothered to tell you.

Jade's eyes closed for her nap before working a night shift at SoundTracks.

April 2003

Chapter Four
Welcome to the Real World

Two years later

It wasn't Miami University, but Grover Community College had all Jade needed. Walking along the small bridge outside that overlooked the theater building, Jade enjoyed the silence on her way to the library after the last class of the day.

"Class was intense today, uh?"

Jade looked over her shoulder and saw two other students from her Fine Arts Appreciation class. She didn't find the class to be intense at all, but having folks warmly approach her on school grounds felt better than the sunny weather outside that day. "Yeah, a little. But I liked it."

The boy laughed and Jade had to remind herself not to bring her shoulders in too close.

"Oh word? That's cool. What's your instrument?"

Reaching up her hand, Jade stopped mid air and chuckled. "Strings. Guitar."

Now that she had a safe place to leave her guitar, Jade didn't need to bring it with her all the time. It had been over a year since she stopped carrying Luxe with her everywhere, but Jade still forgot sometimes.

"Okay. I play the clarinet and my boy here on a voice scholarship. We should get together sometime and jam out."

Jade beamed for a second before her smile disappeared. "That would be cool. I gotta go. See y'all later."

Waving, Jade started to turn away until the boy in front of her called out, "Ayyeee! Have you heard about the new music coffee shop?"

A new what?

"Nah, I ain't heard of that. Where it at?"

He pulled out a yellow flyer from his pocket and handed it to Jade. "They opened earlier this year. Real cool spot."

41

Looking at the flyer, Jade's smile returned. "Thanks."

Hearing the chime of the campus tower clock, Jade made her way to her work study shift at the library.

She made it upstairs with a minute left.

Good thing I ain't have Luxe with me - would've passed out taking the steps to get here.

On her way to the office counter, where everyone had to check in to see which part of the library they were assigned to work in for the night, Jade clipped her school issued name tag badge to the yellow polo shirt she wore. Once she tossed her messenger bag into the designated cubby for her shift, she turned around and nearly bumped into Alice, a shift supervisor.

Why she gotta be so dang close?

Alice was a twice senior, now repeating her senior year at Grover. And the older girl made sure that all the other work studies knew that she was in charge - at least while they worked in the library.

"Thornton, so glad you could make it."

The sarcasm was not lost on Jade. She chose to ignore it, studying her breathing before tucking her shoulder length braids behind her ear. Nodding at the older girl, Jade started to make her way to the main desk to see where she was assigned for the day.

"Where do you think you're going?"

Alice's high pitched voice lacked the more menacing tone Jade assumed she was going for, but since she'd put in her notice at Soundtracks as soon as she began her work study at the library months ago, Jade knew she needed to play along.

This tiny tot twice senior ain't worth losing rent money over.

Jade reminded herself to remain calm as she took a deep breath and faced Alice.

"To the main desk. That's where the assignments are, right?"

"Wrong."

Setting her jaw, Jade was about to speak again but Alice stopped her. "*I'm* the supervisor here, so *I* say where you're assigned."

"Ms. Alice! Is there a problem here?"

Jade let out a sigh of relief when she heard the head librarian's voice. "Hello Mrs. Charles. I was just-"

"Everyone within two meters could hear what you were 'just' doing."

The older woman strolled closer to the two of them, with a clipboard in her hand. She looked up at the clock in the office before glancing down at Alice. "And as of three minutes ago, your shift ended. Good day."

Bringing her lips inward, Jade watched as Alice casted her eyes down and stomped away without a word. Mrs. Charles tapped on the clipboard and smirked.

"Now get to your assigned station young lady. I don't want to miss any more of my stories."

"Yes ma'am. Thank you."

She looked back one last time and smiled while watching Mrs. Charles head into her small private office to watch *Beyond the Gates*.

***

Hours and a short bus ride later, Jade finally arrived home, a modest three bedroom in a not so rough part of town that she shared with Xavier, Lucky's older brother. The summer after their junior year Lucky finally introduced Jade to Xavier at a local PRIDE fest. And with her guardian loudly demanding half of her next paycheck from Soundtracks only days before - Jade wasted zero time in asking to become his roommate. Fortune was definitely on her side too, when he shared that his previous roommate left last month and he was looking for another.

Xavier was hesitant at first about the idea of living with a girl, but Jade won him over that weekend with a few lunches and two months' rent in advance. And after weeks of getting used to each other's quirks and schedules, the two had been living peacefully together ever since.

Once she finished her homework and scrolling through social media, Jade grabbed Luxe from the stand in her bedroom. Strumming each string softly and getting lost into their sounds, Jade almost didn't hear the knock on her door. Xavier stood in the frame of the door, already down to his briefs and socks.

"Hey mana. How was school?"

Jade felt a smile stretch across her lips as she stopped playing.

"It was straight, now that I ain't gotta go back and forth between Soundtracks and my work study no more." Before she could stop herself, Jade whispered, "Is the playing too loud?"

Xavier chuckled, "Girl, how many times I gotta tell you that you can play your guitar as much as you want? The dudes a few condos down have parties until six in the morning sometimes." Leaning in a little he grinned before adding, "Last time one of them was even seen banging on some drums - with his congo stick and maracas out." Xavier winked and Jade giggled.

"Oh, okay. I guess it's an old habit." Jade explained, "I'm used to only playing when I know no one's around."

"It's been years mana! Which brings me to why I'm here." Xavier paused while glancing between her and the door. "If it ain't too weird - could I ask if you mind leaving your door open? I like hearing you play."

Jade always had to close her door when she played Luxe at the house after granny passed. Bringing her eyes up to look at Xavier again, she asked, "Really?"

"Yeah! After dealing with rude ass clients and co-workers at the tattoo shop, it's nice to come home and hear your music. Especially them Spanish guitar songs."

Her cheeks warmed up at hearing his admission, and she swiftly placed Luxe back into a standing playing position. "Really? Oh, um, okay."

Trying to lighten the heavy feeling that began to layer themselves around her heart, Jade added jokingly, "Any special requests?"

Xavier laughed while turning on his heel back to his room. "Ladies choice. Night!"

With Xavier gone, Jade closed her eyes and plucked gently in the second position on Luxe. A discography of songs she'd learned over the years floated through Jade's mind and she mentally slowed down the catalog and selected one of her favorites, *Besame Mucho*. She affectionately called it 'the kissing song', because whenever she played the arrangement it made her imagine what kissing someone must be like.

Not like I'll find out any time soon, but it's nice to think about, I guess.

When she strummed out the last b flat seven and d minor chords, Jade enjoyed the short silence before Xavier's clapping filled the space from across the hall. Her cheeks and hands were warm as Jade got up and closed the door. Making her way back to bed, Jade propped Luxe onto the guitar stand next to the nightstand and turned off the light before climbing into her warm and welcoming bed.

Chapter Five
One Mic

The next morning, Jade got dressed and took out her laptop. While sitting at the kitchenette table, she typed in the name of the coffeeshop that the other kids on campus mentioned.

It seems legit. Maybe I could go and check it out.

"Oh, is that the new spot Clarity's?"

Turning around to see a shirtless Xavier walking past her and into the kitchen, Jade stared at him while he placed a pan on the stove. "I heard some peeps talk about that spot at work last week. Sounds like the place to be these days."

"Yeah, that's what I heard the other day."

Xavier grabbed a bowl from the cabinet and went to open the fridge. "So you gonna go and see what's up?"

Jade stared at the laptop screen and pressed her lips together. "I dunno. I mean, I kinda wanna, but..."

She let the sentence fall while she looked back at Xavier, now cracking two eggs at once into a bowl. He twisted the knob above the stove and grabbed the salt and pepper shakers, sprinkling the spices into it before stirring the contents with a fork.

"What's there to think about? You a musician, right? So go."

The low sizzle from the pan as he poured in the eggs filled the quiet space between them. Jade glanced at the screen again and scrolled down to where she saw the open mic nights tab. Clicking on it, she saw clip after clip of people on stage. Some with only a microphone, but there were others with guitars and even one with a whole band.

I haven't performed in front of a crowd in years. But I could go and enjoy hearing a few live sets, right?

Xavier sat across from Jade with a fresh omelet, cherry tomatoes, and a cup of coffee. He took a sip from the cup and popped a tomato into his mouth before speaking. "What has you slowing your roll on checking out this spot, Jade?"

"I guess...since I don't have anyone to go with - "

He waved a forkful of the fresh omelet in his face, shaking his head as he put it into his mouth. "That's no problem, you know I'll go with you. Just say when."

Jade smiled. "Really? Even if I don't sign up for the open mic, you'd roll through with me?"

"Hell yeah! Me and Raquel would girl! It ain't like I got a man these days to keep me busy - yet."

The two laughed as Xavier continued with another question, "You really think you could go there and not want to take the stage?"

"Open mics ain't really my thing, you know that."

Looking at the laptop one last time, Jade closed out of the website and powered it off before standing and going to the fridge. She almost grabbed the bottle of orange juice before pausing and picking up a bottle of water instead.

"Listen, I don't want to start no beef between us, so I'mma tell you what I think and let you sit with it for a minute." Jade held the cold bottle in her hands and closed her eyes briefly, waiting for Xavier to say more.

"You good Jade. For real. And as much as I hear you strum on your guitar I oughta know." When they stopped laughing, Jade went back to the kitchenette table to sit down. "And maybe open mics ain't "your thing". But you won't know until you try, right?"

When Jade looked over at him, she let out a sigh. "You right."

Finishing the rest of his omelet, Xavier picked up his plate and placed the dishes into the sink. "I know. Just tell me when you wanna go so I can go and see you shine."

***

Thinking about her conversation with Xavier from that morning, Jade finished putting the last of the reference books onto the shelves and went to the main desk to clock out. His question kept playing on loop in Jade's head.

You really think you could go there and not want to take the stage?

It had been years since she had to perform for a crowd, and now that the opportunity to take the stage for herself was here, Jade knew the answer to that question as soon as it came out of Xavier's mouth.

No.

There was no way Jade could pass up the chance to take that stage, especially if it meant she could play and sing whatever songs she wanted to with Luxe in her arms.

I ain't in high school anymore. And I want people to hear me.

She was ready.

First thing the next morning, Jade made sure to make a post on social media about checking out the coffee shop later. And by the time lunch break came around, the post had gotten a few reposts and likes. The first one was from Diamond, who commented with a bunch of hearts and dollar signs. And the others were from Xavier and Raquel, her old co-worker from Soundtracks that she still kept in touch with after quitting. Seeing their digital words of encouragement sealed everything in place.

Guess there's no backing out now.

Work went by in a blur and before Jade had time to try to come up with an excuse to not go, she was back at the condo, standing in front of her bedroom closet.

Xavier and Raquel were pulling out tops and dresses from Jade's merger wardrobe, trying to get her dressed in between their bickering.

"She's going to an open mic Raquel - not some strip joint! Be for real." Turning his nose up at the sequin crop top Raquel held up, Xavier grabbed a pair of black skinny jeans and squealed. "Now THESE are a good start!"

"Ugh! How she gonna perform sitting down in them jeans? Clearly you haven't thought this one through." Raquel said, snatching the jeans out of Xavier's hands and tossing them across the room.

Looking at her friends and fighting back a laugh, Jade walked around them and toward the closet. She reached inside to the back and grabbed the hanger that held the outfit she'd already prepared hours before. The dark blue denim jeans and gold scoop neck top was simple but cute in her opinion as she held it up for them to view.

"I'm wearing this. Y'all can pick my shoes while I go change."

Neither of them said a word as Jade went to the bathroom to shower and get ready. Though when she came back out, she found the duo rummaging under the bed. Raquel's head popped up first, her green eyes almost double in size as she looked at Jade. "Love, at least wear the converses Xavier got you for last Christmas."

In Raquel's hands was a box containing the shoes Xavier gave a few months ago. She liked them, but never saw a reason to wear the kicks on the daily.

Xavier glanced over at the shoes in Raquel's hands, nodding in approval. "Yes! Good to see you got some taste."

"What do you mean?" Raquel stepped closer to Xavier, eyeing him up and down before adding, "You got lucky with these shoes, but trust - that's it *hombre*."

Xavier rolled his eyes before introducing Raquel to the middle finger salute. "I got your hombre right here - hoochie mama!"

Turning to face her way, Xavier pouted out his bottom lip before sneaking a quick peek at the kicks that Raquel raised up toward Jade. "Please? For luck, gordita?"

The hopefulness in his tone tugged at Jade's heartstrings, even as she rolled her eyes from hearing his affectionate nickname for her. The first time he'd called Jade gordita was a few weeks after they'd first met. While out at lunch with Lucky, or Louisa as Xavier called her, he let the name slip out and Jade at first was taken aback. She didn't speak much Spanish, but thanks to the dudes who teased her occasionally in the halls during high school, Jade knew what the word meant. Glancing over to Lucky, who rushed to explain that Xavier meant it as a term of endearment.

"He must really like you, to risk getting cussed out by calling a sista that."

Jade always wanted a nickname, so after Lucky's explanation and taking in the blush on Xavier's cheeks, she smiled at the two of them before going back to her meal.

Bringing herself back to the present, Jade rolled her eyes before accepting the box and removing the kicks. "Okay. Guess a little extra luck couldn't hurt.

***

Once they left the house in Xavier's ride, it didn't take long for them to arrive at the coffee shop. The welcome sign out front was bright, but it was the sign above the building that caught Jade's attention. A black and white portrait of a woman with an afro and serene eyes stared down at her with a caption below that read:

Come on in to Clarity's - The coffee and vintage record shop with Soul.

Taking a picture of the front of the place and removing Luxe from her back, Jade's curiosity was climbing.

So they sell vinyl here too? That's so cool!

From what Jade could see from the brownstone exterior that the place could probably fit a crowd of at least two hundred with no problem. Tea lights and light bulbs were strung at the entrance, with the main double doors held open by large sandwich boards that listed the weekly events and drink specials.

Grabbing Xavier's hand, Jade pushed out a small smile when her friend grinned at her. Vivid blue, purple, and yellow lights were low, though each table had its own tiny lamp that provided just enough light for guests to place their orders without interrupting the atmosphere.

Raquel led them past the barista section, where there was a "help wanted" sign near the cash register, to a space near the stage, which was covered in a variety of thick rugs. There was also a lineup of guitars and ukuleles on display, placed behind the standing microphones. Jade couldn't stop staring as she looked beyond the stage and noticed the framed photos of famous Black performers, from Sister Rosetta Tharpe to Darius Rucker. Finally sitting down and putting Luxe in the empty seat next to her, Jade turned around as she took in more of the new place. When the lights flickered again, a symbol on the wall caught her eye. Jade thought it resembled the rest note that you see on a piece of sheet music. Squinting and confirming, she followed the five lines and four spaces that went around the entire coffee shop. That was when she noticed the accidentals, clefs, and note values spaced out throughout every wall inside the coffee shop.

I am so in love with this place!

"Jade. Jade!"

Hearing Raquel call her name, Jade turned around.

"I saw someone start to set up over there."

Following Raquel's hand as she pointed to the left of the stage, Jade took a deep breath and nodded. Standing, she headed over to the side of the stage and made her way over. Though just as Jade was looking for the sign up sheet, a man out of the corner of her eye picked up a guitar. Curious, Jade made herself busy by admiring the decor again while trying not to get caught being nosy. The man, old enough to be her granddad, started to make the most beautiful guitar she'd ever seen cry. Jade almost didn't want to interrupt him, but she didn't see anyone else that could help her sign up.

"Hey, um, I'm Jade. Jade Thornton. I wanna sign up for a slot in tonight's open mic, please."

The man beamed. "Well, welcome to Clarity's then! The name's Joe. I'll put ya on the list."

While he was writing her name down, Jade continued to stare in awe at the guitar he was just playing.

"See something you like, little miss?"

Realizing that she's been caught drooling over the antique and not liking the 'little miss' remark, Jade's reply was quicker than lightning, " Never thought I'd see a vintage Gibson in this joint – much less someone that knew how to handle it."

Joe let out a booming laugh. "Vintage uh? Tell me – just how do *you* know if this here is vintage?"

Smiling sweetly and locking eyes with Joe, Jade explained, "*Sir* - I may not know much, but I know my strings. That's a late sixties ES-125 Electric Archtop you're strumming on."

Joe's eyes twinkled as he stared at her. In amusement or mischief, Jade couldn't be sure which.

"It's a 1959 to be exact. Joe, leave this child alone!"

Jade turned around and noticed the woman right away from online. She had salt and pepper braids, soft kind eyes, and warm yet stern smile. Her whole vibe seemed to suggest that she was approachable, until you were foolish enough to cross her.

"Woman, don't start on me now! She knows I ain't mean nothin' by it – don't ya lil lady?"

Jade decided to eat a little humble pie before speaking, "It's okay. I guess was staring just a bit too much at her."

"Her?" they both asked.

Smiling sheepishly, Jade started to explain, "I mean, the Gibson. Because it struck me instantly as a classic beauty, so I thought she and her pronouns was best." With both of them staring at her like she'd had three head, Jade rushed out, "Not that I want *your* guitar...I mean I *do*, but - not that I'd – "

Laughing softly, Clarity silenced Jade with a wave. "It's okay baby. We get it. You signed up for tonight?"

"Yes ma'-" Jade started until out of the corner of her eye she noticed Joe shaking his head and making a slicing motion around his neck with his hands. Coughing to hide a laugh she started again.

"Yeah. I signed up."

"Alight. Gone and sit down, and I'll call ya up when it's your turn."

Thanking Clarity, Jade made her way over to the table to where Xavier and Raquel were sitting. The three of them chatted about their days after ordering their drinks and before long Joe appeared on the stage. Hearing him introduce the first performer, a lanky guy with multi-colored locs that went down to his back, Jade couldn't take her eyes off the stage.

She loved the vibe of the coffee shop, each performer that took the mic, but what Jade loved the most was the way Clarity and Joe acknowledged everyone after their set and the crowd. For the first time in quite some time – she wanted to fit in. That's when the butterfly of nerves hit. It has been so long since Jade had allowed herself to want anything. She couldn't help but think the worst. That's what always happened. *Was I really ready to do this again? To try to connect with others again through music?*

The last time she did was in high school, and that didn't end so well. Jade could feel the blood pulsing through her veins, the heat creeping up her chest and spreading its way to her neck and face.

Oh no. No. No, noooooooooh! Big G please, pretty PLEASE do not let me freak and back out now. Please! Please.

After another performer left the stage, Xavier noticed Jade's silence. "Um...You okay love?"

Jade paused in the midst of her inner turmoil and looked her way with panicked eyes and furiously shook her head. Raquel then placed her hand on top of Jade's.

"It's just a little stage fright. You'll be fine!"

"I can't believe I'm saying this, but she's right, mama. Once you start playing Luxe you'll be alright. I promise. "

Still unable to trust herself to speak, Jade gave them both a small smile before turning back towards the stage.

"Thank you Ariel for another great set! All right y'all – we've got a rookie coming to the stage. Hope ya'll remember the house rules, because after meeting her only once my Joe is pretty smitten with her and we're both excited to see what she can do. Welcome to the stage... Jade Thornton!

That's me! Why am I not moving? Girl, get UP!

Her hands were quick to clam up on her as she finally got out of her seat. Before picking up Luxe and walking to the stage, Xavier grabbed her wrist, kissed her briefly on the cheek, and said something to her that she couldn't make out over the thumping of her heartbeat. It must have been funny as hell from the way Raquel had reared her head back and laughed. Jade tried to smile up towards Clarity and Joe, but she felt like she was walking to *The Green Mile* and was sure that she looked constipated.

Finally on the stage, Jade forced herself to take short exhales while she sat down on the stool and got Luxe in position. She thought quickly, *Should I tell them a little about me first? Mention what songs I'm doing? Hell no! Just go up there and get it over with? Yes! Best decision you made all week. Just stare out into the bright lights and for all that you hold dear – do NOT forget the lyrics*!

That last thought caused her to shudder, and Jade silently brought her eyes up to the ceiling and prayed to the Big G that no one noticed.

First up was Seven Oh's 'Glances'. It was her comfort zone cover choice because she knew it inside and out. The thing was not too many folks knew who Seven Oh the group was, much less this song. So she just had to accept that this may not be a good song to start with.

As her left hand found the first position with ease, Jade finally smiled.

Just pretend that you're in your room. Wearing your Whovian slippers and waiting for Raquel to complain about you practicing late instead of going out clubbing with her again.

Just like that, she was somewhere safe. Somewhere comfortable and familiar, playing this song for the fifty-eleventh time.

"I see you...Can you see me?"

Damn. This how I sound with the right equipment? Okaaaay!

By the time she got to the final chorus, her vocal chords had completely relaxed and were more than ready. "I want you! To see me...Cause no matter how much I try not to. I...Love...You..."

After ringing out the last note and chord, Jade quickly remembered where she really was performing. She started to brace herself for the boos and snickers, but there weren't any. Biting the corner of her lip, Jade closed her eyes and got ready to walk off.

Guess they don't want to be rude. That's okay...at least I tried, right?

Despite the situation, Jade couldn't help but smile out at the crowd.

When I get home, I'll be sure to help myself to some of Xavier's 1800 and –

Small finger snapping had begun throughout the coffee shop. Jade squinted to where her crew were seated and saw Raquel wearing the biggest smile she had ever seen on her face while Xavier had both hands in the air – snapping his fingers in Z formation. Planning her self-pity party would have to wait.

Oh my LAWD! I can do my next song – really? Okay!

She had been working on this acoustic version of 'Stayin' Late' for two months now and was excited to share it with someone other than the Nina, Maya and Billie posters hanging up on her bedroom wall. She slowly got into second position on Luxe and softly started the chord progression.

Good! Nice and smooth – just like you practiced.

Apparently this chill yet funky song was what everyone in this joint was waiting on because she could hear rhythmic clapping in the background. Could have just as easily been her heart thumping around in her chest, but Jade was trying her best to be optimistic. Her thoughts were confirmed when she dared to peer out into the crowd again and saw Raquel doing some sort of two step shimming next to Xavier – who at that moment shouted out, "GET IT MAMA!" which got everyone laughing.

For weeks she had been going back and forth about keeping in the rap to this track. Not that it was hard – she just couldn't seem to make it work for her. Knowing all the words to a song and singing them in private is one thing, but to remember all the words when performing in front of a live crowd was a whole different vibe. Then choosing to add your own style to it while not losing the essence of the original track? That part was coming up in twelve counts and she had to decide what to do - fast.

What if I lose 'em? I don't want them to think I'm just a cover girl though. Ugh! Screw this mess, I'mma just run with it.

And run she did. The three bars she added came out like a nice sprint, leaving Jade with plenty of time to fall back into the groove she'd set with this song. Taking her last inhale, Jade closed her eyes and shocked even her damn self with a smooth as silk C octave scale that vibrated from within her chest.

Eyes flying wide open, Jade heard the Gibson she'd been admiring earlier cry out again, and she began to soothe it with some more harmony runs as if she were singing a lullaby to a sleepy child. Slowing down the chord progression until she was able to fade out, Jade tilted her head to where the guitar sound was coming from. To her immediate right, she saw Joe watching her while he strummed chords and notes from what seemed to be at random that matched the sound of her voice.

Whoa! I knew he had to be good, but he makes me sound even better than I thought I could.

She flashed Joe her megawatt of thanks smile before doing one more run and stepping back from the mic.

The applause was thunderous.

Not sure what to do with the attention, Jade slightly bowed and grabbed Luxe to make her way off the stage.

Clarity was at the small steps waiting with a smile that immediately settled Jade's nerves. "You said you know your strings. Glad to see that's true."

"Oooh weee!"

Joe's cheerful voice commanded the space surrounding them as he scooped Clarity into his arms. Swinging her in a full circle, the two laughed as he gently placed Clarity back on solid ground. "I just KNEW you was gonna be good! What'd I say baby? Didn't I tell ya she had it?"

Jade's ears burned from all his praise and she bit her lip while looking away.

"Joe, you embarrassing the child." Clarity said, stepping in front of Jade as she continued, "We hope you'll be back again sometime."

With all the nerve she could muster, she glanced up to Clarity. And when Jade saw how sincere the request was, the question on the tip of her tongue flew out of her mouth.

"Are y'all still hiring?"

The two looked at one another and it was Joe that spoke next, "We is. Two days a week, helping out behind the counter and keeping the stage set and organized. You thank you can do that, lil lady?"

Jade nodded enthusiastically. "Yes, I can."

"Good!" Joe let out a hearty laugh. "Then gone to the counter over there and ask Mariah for an application."

Chapter Six
Found

"I'll have a frappe mocha please." Clarity sweetly requested.

It was Jade's fourth day working at Clarity's that month, and as part of her final barista test, she had to make four random coffee orders. All the previous drink recipes whizzed through her mind, and Jade glanced up to the ceiling in hopes of finding the right one. Hearing Clarity's sparkling laughter, Jade brought her eyes back down to the task.

The barista station looked even smaller as Jade stood behind the counter. She took in all the previously made drinks and rolled her shoulders. "Uh, okay. So..a frappe is made up of..."

She closed her eyes and soon the recipe notes she took during training over the last two weekends came to mind. *Ice, milk, sugar, espresso, and water - got it*!

Grabbing a cup from the stack, Jade got to making the beverage. Once she shook the contents together, she turned to face Clarity again, this time with a smile before placing a black lid on top of the cup. "Here you are. One frappe mocha."

She watched Clarity take a sip of the drink with baited breath.

"It's a little too sweet for my liking, but I'm sure the kids at GCC won't mind." mused before trying the frappe again.

Joe, dressed in a pair of cream colored khakis and a white tank top, made his way over and took the drink out of Clarity's hand. He popped the lid off the cup and gulped down the icy drink.

"It's perfect Jade!" Beaming at her and then Clarity, he continued, "See, told you she'd be a pro by the end of the week!"

Jade glanced down, biting her lip and looking up again at him. "Thanks Joe." Bringing her attention back to Clarity, she quietly asked, "So, I passed, right?"

Seconds passed while Joe and Clarity eyed one another. It was the older woman that broke the silence before taking the cup back from Joe.

"Yes, you can start working behind the counter this weekend."

Joe clapped his hands together and shouted, "Alright now!"

"But only once a week! I want you to keep shadowing the other baristas, and stay on the to-go counter, unless we get slammed." Clarity instructed. Nodding quickly, Jade couldn't stop smiling. "Thank you!"

She looked over at Joe and the two shared a grin. "Can I still practice with Joe in between my shifts?"

The older woman rolled her eyes and let out a chuckle, "As if I could stop you two from playing together. Long as you ain't brushing off your academics to practice with my Joe, it's fine."

Joe leaned back, feigning shock by bringing his hand to his chest. "Now what kind of man would I be if I let baby girl slack off on them books?"

"Mmhmm. I'll remember you said that when y'all get into your groove jamming later." Clarity said, moving over to give Joe a peck on the cheek. Jade watched the interaction between them briefly before looking away.

"The next barista will be in soon, so go ahead and clean up."

"I will. Thank you again!" Jade shouted as Joe and Clarity walked to their office located in the back of the coffee shop.

When she wasn't learning all the drinks and other menu items, along with the other ins and outs of the coffee shop, Jade found herself on stage with Joe as he instructed her on new fingering techniques with the house guitars. She was no slouch when it came to playing the guitar, but with Joe's guidance, Jade learned to play how she felt, not just the way the sheet music told her to.

I feel so connected to Luxe now, like she's the strings to my heart or something...

"Heya Jade!"

Hearing Mariah, the evening barista call out to her, Jade answered cheerfully. "Hey. I just finished cleaning the station."

Jade stepped out of the barista station and watched Mariah put her on an apron and her name tag. She sported a multi-color set of bantu knots that left Jade curious as to what Mariah's curls would look like once she unraveled them later.

"Thanks! See you later."

Walking from behind the station, Jade went to the employee room and grabbed Luxe, as well as her messenger bag. She still had time before jamming with Joe later, so Jade took out her laptop. Logging into her main social media account, she shared her new second job status in a blog post.

I'm not just a musician, but a barista too!

Giggling to herself, Jade continued with her entry, making sure to remind everyone to stop by Clarity's for the next open mic.

"Okay baby girl - you ready to jam?"

Jade looked up to see Joe, now wearing a brightly colored floral button shirt over his white tank top. She had to bite down on her lip to not laugh while asking, "What's with the Hawaiian shirt?"

"Tonight's theme is Honolulu, so I wanted to dress for the occasion. You like it?"

Joe spun around, showing off his shirt, khakis, white knee high socks and black sliders.

"I love it." Jade told Joe, chuckling as she stood up to follow him to the stage.

***

The next week, after her first full shift at Clarity's, Jade waited for Joe on stage. To pass the time, she took out her songbook and looked over some older entries. That was until Jade heard something that sounded like glass hit the floor. Turning around, she saw Mariah and Clarity standing over a table, both looking down at the ground.

"Is everything okay?" Jade asked.

"I'm sorry Ms. Clarity, I didn't see you over the vase and flowers that just arrived. Let me get the broom and dust pan." Mariah said before turning to leave.

Jade hopped off of the stool and sprinted over to see what happened. Before she could reach the table, Clarity held out her hands, signaling for Jade to stop. "Everything is okay. I was on the phone and not watching where I was going, is all."

Glass shards, water, and random flowers were scattered on the floor between them.

"Oh, I see."

The bell to the main entrance ranged and a group of kids walked in. "I'll make sure no one walks this way until Mariah gets back."

Clarity smiled at Jade. "Thanks baby. I'll go on and see what this group wants to drink."

Returning the smile, Jade watched as Clarity went to the front of the coffee shop and welcomed the people that came in. When Mariah returned with a caution sign, broom, and dust pan, Jade began to make her way back to the stage. Until she saw Joe holding what looked like her songbook in his hands.

Oh god! Please don't let that be my book - please!

Jade kept her eyes on Joe as she waved through the empty coffee tables to get back to the stage. Sure enough, the green composition book that she stupidly scribbled 'Musing Notes by Jade' on the front cover was in Joe's hands.

"Hey! I didn't know you were back." Jade said brightly. Her hands immediately went to take the book out of Joe's hands. "I'll put this..."

Joe sidestepped Jade, his eyes never leaving the pages of her book. With her heart jackhammering wildly against her ribcage, Jade managed to whisper out, "Joe? Can I have my book back please?"

"Why you ain't tell me you can write too?"

Afraid of what Joe was reading - or thinking about her in that moment - Jade chose to answer jokingly, "Well, most college students can read, and write Joe..."

One look at him told Jade that that was the wrong approach.

"You know what I mean. Why you ain't tell me you also had songwriting in your bag of skills?"

"I-I dunno..."

Jade's throat went dry as Joe stared at her. Gone was the usually mischievous and warm hearted man she'd come to know over the last few months. Joe's stern voice asked, "Why you do that there?"

"Do what?"

"Try to be funny instead of answering the question I ask ya?"

Jade blinked at Joe before she tried to speak again. Knowing that he wanted an honest answer left her stumbling over what to say. She finally decided to not say anything and Jade's shoulders slumped before she looked down at her feet.

"I ain't mean to embarrass you baby girl, but Jade... These here lyrics are good."

Hearing praise instead of a lecture, Jade cautiously brought her eyes back to Joe's.

"Really?"

"Yeah baby girl! You got some good hooks and stuff in these pages!"

Jade's beamed.

He really said I was good? Really?

Joe's praise was short lived as he asked, " But why the first time I'm seeing this - by accident, no less? Why you writing all this down in your book and not telling no body?"

When Jade went back to looking at her feet, crossing one pair of kicks over the other, Joe hit her with another round of questions. "Why you trying to hide what you feel? You thank that's what all them other songwriters out there doing? Hiding from everybody and keeping their words tucked away in a book?"

When she didn't answer, Joe looked at the composition book again and handed it to her. He waited for her to look him in the eye. "You got a gift. More than that - you is dedicated to learning how to better yourself. A lot of folks say they can do what you do, but they never do. But I see you Jade, and as much as it pains me to say it, you ain't ready."

Jade looked up at Joe with her mouth open. "W-what? But you just said-"

"Being gifted and being ready to go into the world with your gifts are two different thangs. "

She glanced down at her composition book.

"How long you had that there book?" Joe asked

Jade looked at him again and answered slowly. "For a few years."

"And I bet ain't nobody seen a word in there 'cept you. Right?"

She thought back to her junior year of high school, when Nashone read out loud a line from the same book.

I about bit his head off then. Maybe Joe's right and I just can't do this songwriting thing.

"Now, ain't no reason to be looking all long in the face. You just need to be honest with ya self. Why you write in that book and not say what you feeling?"

Jade knew the answer to that, and she wished like hell it wasn't true. But since walking into Clarity's, she finally felt safe enough to say so out loud. "I'm sacred."

Joe stared at Jade for a beat before motioning for her to sit on the carpet of the stage before sitting across from her. "Whatcha got to be scared?"

The years of being an easy target for folks to make fun of flashed through Jade's eyes. Memories she wanted to forget of family members teasing her and classmates clowning her as she passed them in the hallways. No matter how hard she tried to forget, Jade knew the feeling that came afterwards. And she hated it.

"I'm scared to share what I feel...cause when I tried to in the past, people just laughed. And I don't want to try to fit in anymore only to be let down or hurt again."

Joe slowly nodded. "So you keep writing your thoughts in that book, getting it all just right. For what?"

She brought her eyes up to Joe, confused.

"Putting yourself out there ain't never easy, even when you get to my age." Seeing Joe puff out his chest and letting out a loud sigh, Jade giggled.

"But I'mma let you in on a secret. You don't do it for the crowd - you do it for *you*." Jade opened her mouth, but Joe waved a hand in the air as he went on, "Yeah, it sholl is nice when what you have to say is well received. But life don't work like that baby girl. Putting yourself out there in this big ole world to get hurt is part of the life experience."

Jade tilted her head and fought hard to not pout, "Even if hurts?"

"*Especially* if there's a chance you'll get hurt. That's called being brave. And the ones that get it will come to appreciate you more for putting yourself out there."

Silence filled the cafe as Jade thought over his words.

"From what I read in your book, you've got plenty to say. So, if you want a crowd to hear it - you gots to be brave and share it with them baby girl."

Jade looked over at Joe and let out a sigh. "I hear you Joe, but that sounds hard as hell to do." Realizing the words that came out of her mouth, Jade's eyes widened as she sputtered out, "I-I'm sorry! I meant to say - "

Joe's robust laughter stopped Jade mid sentence. She felt him looking at her and peaked over to see the mischievous grin she came to admire on his face. "I know what you meant. And I ain't saying it gotta be today, or even tomorrow. Just know that when you ready, you have a space to share what's on your mind, okay?"

Tears stung her eyes as Jade nodded. Before they fell, she turned to the side and blinked them away.

***

Clarity's was packed that night, and Jade wasn't the least bit worried. She had been practicing the new song with Joe for weeks now and was ready to share it with the crowd. With Joe signing in and explaining the house rules to a few new musicians, Jade lowered Luxe's saddle a bit, perking her ears until she found the sound needed for the first song. Movement then caught the corner of her eye and Jade watched Clarity walk up the small steps to the stage. She held the microphone in front of the growing crowd.

"Coming to the stage is our very own Jade Thornton!"

The thunderous claps that followed made Jade grin while walking onto the stage.

"Now, she ain't a stranger to the stage, but my Joe tells me that she has an original to share with y'all tonight. Is that alright?"

Someone shouted, "Okay songstress!" and laughter erupted throughout the crowd.

Looking at Clarity, who chose to don a sky blue wrap around dress for the night, Jade lowered her head when the older woman walked over. Feeling Clarity's lips against her forehead, Jade closed her eyes and welcomed the sweet floral scent that lingered from Clarity to her nose.

"Go on baby, play your song." Clarity said with a smile.

The humming of the live microphone made its way to Jade's ears, bringing with it the nervousness she thought she had left behind for the night. Strapping Luxe around her neck, Jade leaned into the mic.

"Hey y'all, thank you for the warm welcome."

A few folks clapped and yelped as she continued. "Like Clarity said, I've got an original for y'all, and I hope you like it. But just in case it's not what you wanna hear tonight, don't worry - I'll be sure to give y'all a cover before I roll out."

The crowd laughed, giving Jade just enough time to check the strings on her guitar. When each string ranged through clearly, she took a deep breath and hummed low into the mic.

"Oh shit! She 'bout to get nasty y'all!"

Well, if I was a little nervous before, I'm fo sho big nervous now!

Jade let her trembling fingers do the talking before she joined the instrumental arrangement. *"The night rain against my skin...That's what I think love must be like..."*

Moving along through the first verse, Jade remembered Joe's advice after he found the song in her composition book.

If you want a crowd to hear it - you gots to be brave and share it with them.

With the house lights dimmed low, and the tealights shimmering above, Jade relaxed into playing her first original song. Near the ending, she kept the finger plucking light and steady, letting her voice smoothly sang out, *"I must be in love...with the rain..."*

Releasing her right hand from Luxe, Jade stared out past the house lights. Someone in the first few rows stood up and clapped before several others joined them.

Why do they look so familiar?

Jade kept her eyes on the guy in what looked like a three piece suit. Hearing steps behind her, Jade turned to see Clarity and Joe making their way to her with smiles on their faces. Wordlessly, Clarity wrapped an arm around Jade and kissed her cheek, as Joe looked on. When he sent an exaggerated head nod to her, Jade burst out laughing before swinging Luxe around to her back and engulfing both of them in a big hug.

Chapter Seven
(More Than) Friendly Connections

As she promised, Jade finished her set with two covers - the first cover song she'd ever sung at Clarity's, along with a surprise cover for Clarity. Joe stayed on stage and the two of them got the crowd to help in singing an extended Stevie Wonder version of Happy Birthday. Seeing the shock and joy in her boss's eyes as they serenaded her with the crowd left Jade blinking back happy tears.

"You ain't thank I'd forget the day the love of my life was born, did ya?" Joe asked Clarity after they left the stage.

Jade couldn't take her eyes off the two, as Joe pulled Clarity close and they gently brushed their noses together.

"I should've known you would've had something up your sleeve, since we agreed to not get each other no gifts this year."

Clarity held Joe's face in between her hands and showered him with kiss after kiss.

I would love to have something like that someday.

Before she could think more about it, Jade spotted someone in a dark three piece suit walking out of the unisex restrooms. Her eyes went wide as she turned away.

I know that wasn't who I thought it was!

"Oh baby girl! Is our love too much for you?" Joe teasingly asked.

Counting to three in her head, Jade faced Clarity and Joe again, forcing a smile onto her face. "No, I love seeing y'all together."

Her heart rate spiked as the last person she expected stood behind Joe and cleared their throat.

"Long time, no see Jade."

With nowhere to run or hide, Jade coughed before speaking, "Um, h-hey."

Joe looked behind him at the guy in the suit. She saw his eyes taking in her friend from high school and Jade used that time to work up the nerve to make introductions. "Clarity, Joe, this is Nashone. We went to school together."

Nashone's eyes briefly looked away from Jade before he smiled widely at Joe and Clarity. "You're the owners of Clarity's Coffee shop?"

Joe was a few inches shorter than Nashone, but Jade watched as he squared up to Nashone. "Who's asking?"

"Yes, my husband and I opened this cafe earlier this year." Clarity said, reaching out to take one of Joe's hands into hers. "We'll let y'all get reacquainted."

"But I wanna know-" Joe started.

Jade fought a smile when she noticed Clarity glance at Joe and then tilt her head. When she went to look at Nashone, Jade locked eyes with him and quickly looked away.

"Joe, let's go check and see if the next performer is ready, okay?" Clarity suggested.

Not waiting for him to say a word, Clarity led Joe away, and Nashone walked closer to Jade. "He must not trust a suit and tie kinda guy."

For years, Jade wondered what she would say to Nashone if she ever saw him again, and now that he was standing in front of her, Jade's brain seemed to stop working. Every slick remark she had carefully crafted just for this moment failed to come to her. So she did the only thing she could do - Jade turned her heel and began heading in the opposite direction.

"Really Jade?"

Hearing Nashone chuckle, Jade whirled around and found him shaking his head. "I see you ain't changed since high school."

Anger rose to Jade's cheeks, turning her body into a furnace.

I know he ain't finna try and act like we good right now!

A new cutting statement ziplined through her mind, and Jade snatched it as though it were a lifeline. Pushing air out from her nose, she glared at Nashone. "I see you still relying on your looks to get by. Tell me, how much did that sucker suit set you back?"

When he tilted his head back and laughed, Jade wanted to scream.

My insults still don't work on him. Damnit!

"I've missed you."

Hearing his voice drop an octave, Jade tried to calm the butterflies that had begun floating around in her stomach.

"Your disses - I mean. I missed hearing them." Nashone added quickly, causing his voice to go up half a pitch.

Looking at him, Jade noticed Joe and Clarity watching them. And as much as she wanted to test out what he just said, Jade didn't want to have all eyes on her right now. Sighing, she rolled her eyes, "Why are you here?"

"I wanted to see the open mic talent."

Jade stepped up to him and she could have sworn that he puffed out his chest, bringing theirs closer than she meant to.

Immediately stepping back, she asked, "No, why are you here? Back in town?"

Nashone met her stare, before lowering his gaze. She bit the corner of her lip as she waited for him to speak, but he took his time raising his eyes back up. Smiling, Nashone finally answered, "I got an internship that's nearby."

When Jade said nothing, he continued with a scoff. "I ain't know you'd be here. If I did..."

All her good sense shouted for Jade to not take the bait, but when Nashone smirked, she blurted out, "What? What would you have done if you knew I was here?"

"I would've came through sooner."

Squinting her eyes shut, Jade counted to five before slowly opening one and wanted to groan out loud. *Yep, he's still standing in front of me. This is not a dream. Damn!*

"Let's try this again. Hey Jade!"

She looked at Nashone like he'd just grown three extra heads.

"Come on, Jade! We were friends once, weren't we?"

Jade locked eyes with Nashone, answering flatly. "Yeah, once."

"So let's try to start over again."

She seriously considered walking away, but remembered that Joe and Clarity were watching them. If she did that, Jade knew they'd come looking for her and she was not up for talking about how she lost touch with Nashone back in high school."

"Fine. Hello Nashone."

He had the nerve to look offended. "Dang, you talk like that to all your friends?" When Jade didn't respond, he tried again. "Okay, so...how you doing?"

"Good. You?"

"Been pretty good for a while now. You must be a regular here."

Jade bit the inside of her jaw, already done with whatever this was supposed to be and the former friend in front of her. *This is feeling too much like a social experiment.*

"Guess you must be comfortable performing solo."

Memories of calling him and getting no answer flashed through Jade's mind before she finally answered. "What, you want to take credit for making that happen?"

Nashone glanced away before looking at Jade again, "Jade, can we talk? For real?"

"I thought that's what we're doing."

Hearing him sigh, Jade watched him take a step closer and extended his hand before pausing and let it fall to the side before clearing his throat. "Look, I know what happened in high school was messed up, but if you got time, I wanna try to explain."

She didn't want to admit it, but a part of Jade did want to know what happened back then. And if she left tonight, she'd always be left wondering why.

Suppose it couldn't hurt to hear what he has to say.

"Well, I just finished my set for tonight. How do you take your coffee?"

He smiled as Jade briskly walked over to the barista station. Up ahead Jade watched Clarity step over to Mariah. Strolling over behind the barista counter, Clarity shooed Mariah away while putting on an apron.

Guess there's no way I can get out of not sharing more details about Nashone tonight...

"Everybody been asking me when you going to release your album Jade. Guess they really like that original song."

Normally hearing praise from Clarity would leave Jade doing a cute two-step, but with Nashone being close by, all she could do was smile.

"So, whatcha drinking tonight?" Clarity asked Nashone, never once taking her eyes off of Jade.

Nashone glanced at the drink menu behind Clarity and answered, "Can I get a red eye please?" He turned to Jade. "Which drink you want?"

Jade didn't have to answer him, as Clarity beat her to it. "She'll have hot water with honey and two lemon slices."

With Nashone now looking between the two of them, Clarity laughed, "She's my newest part timer, and the only one on staff that don't drink coffee."

Nashone joined Clarity in another chuckle before she went to make their drinks. "How you work at a coffee shop and don't drink coffee?"

Jade kept her eyes straight ahead until Clarity came back with their drinks.

The sooner I get this over with, the sooner I can go home and watch whatever Telenovela Xavier has on at home.

She walked away while Nashone paid for his coffee and scanned the coffee shop to find them a place to sit. Seeing one of the smaller tables close to the stage but only a few feet away from the second exit door, Jade made a beeline for the spot before anyone else could claim the space. He didn't even fully sit down before Jade got straight to the point, "Okay, why did you not show up for the recital?"

Nashone's head jerked back, "You not gonna let me sit down and think of what to say first?"

"You've had years to think about this, and I have somewhere else I wanna be."

Sighing, Nashone leaned forward in the chair and met Jade's glare.

"I was just, I dunno...damn, I was hoping this would go down differently."

When Jade went to leave, he spoke again.

"My Pops works - worked in construction back in the day. He finally had to retire after a hard fall on site. When we first got to town, he told us things would be all good once the worker's comp came through. But the weekend before our recital, I got home and all our stuff was already packed and going into a U-Haul."

So, they moved cause his daddy lost his job?

Jade could relate. If it wasn't for Granny Gladys' insurance policy, she was sure that she would've had to bounce around too. Just like her cousins and everyone else in their family did. But that wasn't what bothered her about Nashone leaving, and now that she was faced with that fact, she had to choose. Holding the cup full of warm water in both her hands, Jade looked down and thought over what to say.

"That's why I texted you what I did." Nashone finished, before taking a sip of his coffee.

She remembered seeing his last one word text that day. And looking across from Nashone now, only told her one thing - she wasn't over it. Every time since her recital, Jade avoided playing her guitar with anyone else. Because of what happened all those years ago. With that reality staring Jade hard in the face, this felt like the best time to lay everything bare. She put down the cup, blinking her eyes to stop the tears that she felt coming to the surface.

"I called you." Jade whispered. "I texted and called, and you never answered. Why?"

Out of the corner of her eye, Jade saw Joe begin his closing ritual of turning on the bright stage lights and checking the patio area. She could feel Nashone staring at her, but Jade wouldn't look at him.

This is dumb! What was listening to him now supposed to do for me anyways?

Standing up, Jade made her way back to front to get her things, but hearing Nashone called out her name, she stopped.

"I got your messages. But...but I ain't know what to say."

She finally forced herself to look at him. And seeing him peer down into his drink, Jade did something she hadn't done before. In those brief seconds, she thought about how things must've been from Nashone's point-of-view. For years she could only feel and think about how everything was for her, but watching him after all this time and hearing the pain in his voice, Jade realized that maybe the duet recital that didn't happen didn't just suck on her end. Which is why she chose to not diss Nashone again.

Instead, Jade said what she wanted to hear from him back then.

"I guess saying goodbye was too hard."

"Jade, you gotta know - I didn't want to. For the first time ever, I had a real friend. You know, someone I could kick it with and just be myself."

There was something in Nashone's eyes when he met her stare. Something that made her want to believe that he wasn't fronting. Jade didn't notice the first tear when it fell— not until the little droplet wet the tips of her fingers. She quickly reached up to wipe her face, turning away.

"Can I come by and see you again?" Nashone asked.

With her heart swaying inside her chest, Jade nodded before finally walking away.

***

The next day, classes were canceled due to campus building renovations, so Jade went to work early at Clarity's. She smiled at Joe, seeing him take out the house instruments. "Can I help?"

He looked over at her, wiping a sheen of sweat from his balding head. "Why yes you can help. Matter of fact, I'mma gone 'head and rest while you bring out the rest of the equipment."

Jade laughed as she watched him take a seat at one of the front row tables and take a swig from the bottle of water. "Whatcha doing here so early 'fo any ways? Your shift don't start for another five hours."

"I know, but since I ain't have no classes today, I thought I'd come in and shadow Mariah. 'Til I feel more confident in a few of the house coffee specials."

Joe nodded as he took another sip of his water. "Good."

More minutes passed before Jade got all the house instruments out of the storage room and onto the stage. Over the last month, she learned from a few other performers how Joe liked to have the speakers and cords set up, so Jade went ahead and got those in place.

Must be doing alright, he ain't said nothing yet.

It wasn't until Jade started to position the speakers on the stage did she hear Joe's booming voice. "Now you ain't got to do all that. Gone and pick a string to practice on."

"I can do it." Jade offered, making sure to use her knees to bend and bring the heaviest of the speaker toward the middle of the stage.

Soon it felt lighter and Jade looked to see Joe lift the other end, grinning, "I can't have the missus seeing you do this here by yo'self. You gonna get me in trouble."

Once the speakers were in their usual spots, Jade started to leave the stage.

"You don't like the house strings?" She heard Joe say.

Turning around, Jade looked at him before asking, "Why you think that?"

"Most folks wouldn't hesitate to pick up and play the house instruments, but not you. What, you only got eyes for my Gibson?"

Jade laughed, "I do have eyes for her, but she ain't mine. Luxe is. I just like to play her, that's all."

Joe sat back down in the front row, keeping his eyes on Jade. "How long you had your Luxe?"

Jade felt her cheeks rise as she remembered that summer years ago. "My granny got it for me on my 13th birthday."

Just as quickly, the years since granny Gladys' passing flashed through her mind and Jade's smile disappeared. "That was eight years ago."

"I see." Joe's eyes went from Jade to her guitar before resting on Jade again. "Well, if you ever need a backup, or wanna test out the new strings for me sometime, you're always welcome to."

"Thanks Joe."

***

An hour passed before the front door to the cafe swung open. Jade stopped her scale practice and smiled widely at seeing Mariah bounce inside.

"You coming for my job, newbie?"

Jade shook her head, "Girl please, I'll never be as good as you are making all those drinks."

"I know that's right!"

The two shared another laugh as Mariah pulled her braids back into a low bun. "Besides, it looks like you 'bout to get signed soon."

Scrunching up her eyebrows, Jade turned to face her, "What you mean?"

"You ain't gotta front with me Jade. I'm happy for you!" Seeing the confusion on Jade's face, Mariah asked, "So, you really not gonna be signing with Guerilla Records?"

"Guerilla Records? I doubt anyone there knows who I am, much less would wanna sign me."

From what Jade knew about the record label, they were heavily rap based. With their major artists having just as many felonies as hit records. The few female rappers that did sing from time to time didn't look or sound anything like her either.

Mariah stared at Jade for longer than Jade liked before speaking again. "The guy you was with the other night? Some of the kids from campus say he works for Guerilla."

Jade's eyes widened while Mariah continued, "Before your set, he was talking to some of the other musicians and gave them his business card. We thought that's why he was talking to you last night."

Nashone works for Guerilla?

"You really didn't know?" Mariah asked. Turning to grab her apron, the older girl walked behind the counter, tying the apron around her waist. "Forget I said anything."

Jade wished she could forget, but after thinking back to everything last night and Nashone's answer for being in town - it all made sense. His response to her question about being back in town and rolling through Clarity's. And when Nashone asked if he could stop by again - it wasn't just to see her.

I let myself think he was serious about being friends again. So stupid!

Slumping her shoulders, Jade made her way behind the counter to start work.

***

The night crowd filled into Clarity's once the sun went down, leaving Jade with a decision to make.

Should I stay and see if Nashone shows up? Or go home?

She glanced around the coffee shop and listened to the small talk between the customers that mingled with the low lo-fi music playing in the background. It had been a minute since Jade spent time with Xavier, or Diamond and her nephew Dimar, so she took out her phone and sent each of them a quick text to see what they were up to.

"Aye, it's that A&R dude from Guerilla Records!"

Whipping her head in the direction that the excited voice came from, Jade looked on as Nashone strolled through the coffee shop. He extended a hand out to some regulars and they accepted it, pulling him into a quick hug before letting. Nashone was dressed in a pair of acid washed jeans and a blue shirt.

Guess he trying to fit in with the crowd.

"Hey. What's good y'all?" she heard Nashone say before smiling at the group. Everyone around him started talking all at once and he put a hand up in the air to get them to stop. "Yo, this ain't no press conference y'all, chill out."

Jade listened as the growing group around him laughed and shook her head.

"We heard you went to school here back in the day, is that true?"

She tried to look away, but seeing Nashone's downcast eyes, Jade couldn't as he spoke again, "Yeah, yeah. I did a year at Northern Lights."

"That's how you know Jade?"

Nashone's smirk was in full effect when he nodded. "Yeah. We went to school together then." Before anyone could ask him more questions, Nashone asked, "Is she here now?"

Seeing the group turn to look at the barista station, Jade quickly squatted behind the counter.

Damn! I knew I should've asked to leave early today.

The sound of wind chimes startled Jade from her thoughts, sending her bottom to the ground when she jumped from the noise. Eyes wide, Jade listened closely until the realization that the sound was coming from her front pocket kicked in. She reached into her pocket and took out her phone after seeing Xavier's name on the screen.

"Hey! You texted me - what up?" Xavier said cheerfully.

"Oh, yeah. Hey." Jade looked out in front of the station for any customers before whispering, "I ain't seen you in a minute and wanted to know if you had plans tonight."

Xavier's rich laugh came through the line, "Glad you hear you ain't forget about me! And as a matter of fact, I do have plans tonight - probably tomorrow morning too. So don't wait up for me mana!"

"TMI Xavier! But thanks for the heads up." Jade said before ending the call.

While putting her phone away, she heard a cough from behind and looked up to see Nashone staring down at her. "Ain't it against company policy to be on your phone while you should be working?"

Not returning his smile, even though seeing it directed her way sent Jade's butterflies humming around in her stomach. Fixing her lips into a straight line, she stood and faced Nashone at the barista counter. "That may be the policy over at Guerilla Records, but Clarity is cool with it."

Nashone looked away before meeting Jade's stare. She didn't give him a chance to speak as she continued, "Were you going to tell me where you worked? Or just dip out again once I found out from all your new fans?"

Hearing Nashone mutter under his breath, Jade snapped, "Order something or bounce."

"Why you always talking to me like I'm a scrub?" Nashone finally got out. Jade narrowed her eyes and he rushed out, "I was gonna tell you. The first night I was in here and saw you on stage. But, um...I-"

"You what Nashone?"

"I-I got distracted. Seeing you on stage. It made me think about the last time I heard you play. And how I messed up things between us."

Meeting his stare, Jade couldn't hear anything else. Not the music playing throughout the coffee shop, or the people around them. Nashone placed a hand on top of the desert counter and Jade's hand itched to reach out and make contact.

"I'm sorry Jade. For real." Jade blinked her eyes several times as Nashone went on, "I am sorry that I couldn't be there for you back then."

Her hand slowly made its way to Nashone's and she placed it on top of his. She felt her heartbeat moving in double time when Nashone flipped his hand over and brushed his thumb against Jade's. Hearing him finally say what she had wanted to hear for years now made Jade want to do something she'd only dreamed of. Her eyes took in Nashone's full lips and left Jade pulling in her bottom lip.

Suddenly, the house lights flashed brightly before dimming down around them, leaving only the tealights and stage lights a full watt.

"Jade, you need a 15 minute break?"

She turned around to the sound of Clarity's voice and found both Clarity and Mariah looking her way. Nashone coughed, and Jade tightly shut her eyes before quickly glancing his way.

"Yeah. I do."

Chapter Eight
Buys and Sells

Jade avoided Mariah's stare as she walked past her and Clarity from behind the barista station. Now without the barrier between them, Jade grew more nervous with each step she took toward Nashone. Standing in front of him, she counted slowly to three before asking, "So, what do you do at Guerilla?"

Nashone grinned and reached out for Jade's hand. She didn't have a chance to pull away, as more customers suddenly made their way to the counter to order drinks and desserts before the open mic sessions started. With her heart now stuck in her throat, Jade closed her eyes and let Nashone lead them from the crowd. When they came to a stop, she opened them and noticed that they were at the same table that they talked at the other day.

The smell of something woodsy yet citrusy reached Jade's nose and she felt Nashone's chest bump into her shoulder.

He smells so good.

Looking up and seeing Nashone still grinning her way, on top of that scent that followed, left Jade lost for words. So she focused on watching as he pulled out her seat and waited for her to sit. Jade tilted her head when she sat, her eyes getting lost in the sight of Nashone's hands. With the musicians on stage strumming a Spanish guitar solo, her mind immediately conjured up ways she wished he would introduce himself using those big and well cared for looking hands.

Oh my god! Jade, what is wrong with you?!

It was almost like Jade had unlocked all the secret thoughts she ever had about Nashone. And as hard as she tried to tuck them away, they refused to go back to the corners of her mind. Her entire face felt warm and that warmth started to travel throughout her body, racing to a place Jade never dreamed she'd want it to. Nashone finally sat across from her and leaned in to be heard over the music. But it was no use, Jade couldn't focus on the words that were coming out of his mouth. All she wanted - needed - in that moment was to let this new warmth continue its journey south. It was so close, all she had to do was stay in tune with the sound of the Spanish guitar and the thought of Nashone's lips, hands, and scent.

Oh, please! Just let me...

The sweet Spanish guitar solo ended and was replaced by the loud cheers and chatter from the crowd, bringing her back to reality. Jade wanted to cry out loud as she felt the warm sensation grow cold and all but disappear from her body.

"Jade. Jade?"

Hearing Nashone's voice call out to her, Jade refocused her attention on him.

"You good?"

Not trusting herself to speak, Jade nodded, and Nashone spoke again. "I did tell you the truth about my job that first night. Well, a little."

From the corner of her eye, Jade spotted Joe glance in her direction as he walked over to the stage and she cleared her throat.

"What do you mean?"

"Well, last year I started interning for Guerilla Records. But then an opening came up for an A&R assistant and I applied. I've been doing it for the last seven months."

Without his cologne lingering in the air or the sound of strings to preoccupy her thoughts, Jade started to understand more of what Nashone was saying. And just as quickly, her defense walls went up in response.

"So, you help find talent for the record company? That's why you really wanted to see me again, isn't it?"

A part of her hoped he would say no, but when Nashone sighed, Jade knew the answer. Pushing her chair back, she was about to stand until he called out to her with both his hands out in front of Jade.

"I know how it looks, but Jade - regardless of what is - what happened between us, I still think this could be a great opportunity for you."

Remembering that she had an audience and was still at work, Jade took a deep breath and released it before asking, "How?"

Nashone started to lean over the table but after seeing Jade's unchanged expression, he returned to his side. "Guerilla Records has artists, but what we need now are musicians and songwriters. Creative folks with serious musicality that can be raw, edgy, and unexpected."

Jade said nothing as Nashone briefly looked down and then back at her. "You've always had all of that, Jade. I just want to give you a chance to finally show everyone."

Folding her arms across her chest, Jade finally spoke. "Let me translate – ya'll have fine ass female artists who got some club tracks out and now your record label is looking to try and capitalize on their popularity by having them work with musicians - like me- who can give them a new sound from behind the scenes."

She watched Nashone as he thought over everything she said.

The second he opens his mouth and tries to sugarcoat what I just said, I'm out.

Nashone cleared his throat before leveling his eyes with Jade's.

"Yeah. I'll keep it one hundred—we've got artists that sell. But they can only sell one kind of sound and Guerilla Records wants to change that. So, I am offering you a chance, Jade. Take it, and if everything goes well, three years from now, Guerilla could foot the whole bill for your first extended play release."

Damn.

Jade thought for sure that he would try to deny what she said, but he didn't. She stared at him hard and came to a new realization. This was not the same Nashone Daniel's from high school. He was actually putting in the work – paying his dues to get to the top and not relying on just his good looks. She had to acknowledge and respect that. Then Jade thought about the offer that he just gave her.

Three years.

One thousand and ninety-five days with a record label and playing by their rules. Three years of working with the same kind of chicks Jade tried to avoid all throughout high school and now snickered at when they pranced into Clarity's and purr their vaginas out on stage.

Could I really do it?

For the chance at unlimited studio time – with high end equipment and the creative freedom to finally release an EP that could open more doors for her career?

"Okay. What exactly would you need me to do?"

***

All Jade could think about during her shift at the GCC library that Monday was what Nashone laid out to her at Clarity's last week. He wanted to bring the Director of A&R to Clarity's later that week and Jade couldn't front - she was nervous.

I just started performing in front of folks again...am I doing too much?

After Nashone left Clarity's that night, Jade shared with Clarity and Joe his offer. And although they both had concerns about this offer and Guerilla Records, the two eventually congratulated Jade on the opportunity.

"Just make sure to not sign nothin' without lookin' it over with us first, baby girl." Joe told her.

She tried to focus on putting the returned books back on their proper shelfs, but Jade's head was full of chord progressions and song lyrics from her book. *O-M-G! In just one more day, I'll be performing with Luxe for Guerilla Records!*

Chapter Nine
A Man's World

"So tonight it's going down? You're really gonna perform for Guerilla Records at Clarity's?" Xavier asked for the second time that day.

Jade's hands shook slightly as she put Luxe into the hard case and closed it. "Yes, it's tonight."

A few days ago, Xavier had to have his ankle put in a cast, thanks to a stress fracture from working out. Jade knew he was going stir crazy from having to wear a walking boot, so she tried to be patient with his back to back questions. She watched as Xavier sat up on the couch in their condo and slowly moved his casted ankle up onto the arm of the couch. Jade could feel him giving her outfit a quick assessment. "So, why are you wearing that?"

Rolling her eyes as Xavier laughed, Jade sent a middle finger salute in his direction with her free hand. "I'm wearing what I always wear." She watched him open his mouth and quickly added, "Besides, I have to work right after I take the mic and that halter top dress you left out on my bed ain't exactly my normal barista attire."

Xavier sighed, "Whatever! Just make sure to call me and let me know how it goes, chicka."

Jade made her way to the door and turned to smile at her friend. "I will. See you later!"

***

If I see a crowd of peeps before going on stage right now, I think I'll pass out or something.

Her stomach churned all the way to the coffee shop, so when she got off the bus and made it to Clarity's, Jade made sure to use the back entrance. The smell of roasted coffee beans and sweets welcomed her, calming her stomach a little. Until she looked across the shop and saw Nashone with an entourage of folk about to sit down. They weren't exactly in the front row, but Jade had been performing enough at Clarity's to know that she'd be able to see them a little bit beyond the stage lights.

Come on Nashone! Why you ain't get them in seats further away?!

Everything around her started to sound too loud. From the espresso machine, to the normally relaxing house music that played inside the coffee shop. The voices that Jade heard in the space clashed with one another, causing her to take slower steps toward the employee room behind the barista station. Each step felt heavier than the last and Jade started to feel lightheaded.

"Hey baby girl!" Joe boomed from behind.

When she turned to the sound of his voice, Jade saw Clarity walking up to her. "Jade! Nashone just -" Clarity stopped speaking and looked at Joe. "Let's get you something to drink. Joe, take Luxe right quick."

Jade's head felt heavy when she looked at Clarity. "I'm...okay."

Joe was by her side and Jade wanted to sigh in relief when he took the hard case out of her hands. "Baby girl, you a lotta thangs, but I ain't never pegged you for no liar." She stared at Joe and heard him whisper to Clarity, "It done finally happened. Told you this was too much too soon for her!"

Clarity stepped in front of her, and Jade sent the older woman a smile.

"I just-just need to sit down. I think."

"Okay. I'll bring you something to drink." Before Jade could thank her, Clarity continued, "But if you still feeling woozy after twenty minutes, Joe's going to take you home."

Whipping her head toward Clarity, Jade winced from the pain but sputtered out, "What? No! I still have - "

She watched as Clarity's eyes narrowed and locked onto hers and the older woman spoke again, more sternly than before. "What you have to do is take care of yourself. And as your employer, I refuse to let you push yourself to any extremes."

"That's right! Them folks from Guerilla Records can wait. Your health more important than them, baby girl."

Looking at them both, Jade saw that nothing she said would change their minds. Once she made it to the employee room, Joe offered her a seat before opening the large window and leaving. When he returned, he handed Jade a mug with the coffee shop's name written in bold red and black script.

"The missus says you have to drink this. All of it Jade." Joe instructed.

When she took the cup from him and caught a whiff of the contents, Jade immediately turned her nose and held the cup away.

"What is it?" she asked.

"She called it 'The Songstress Elixir.'" Joe told her.

Jade's lips turned downward as she spied the golden liquid inside the cup. It was warm at least, so she pinched her nose with her free index finger and thumb before gulping down the contents of the cup. Her throat immediately went numb, but other than that, Jade was fine.

"How you feel? Still lightheaded?"

Her eyes widened. "How did you know that?"

Joe cocked his head to the side and smirked, "You thank you the only person to come in here with a case of stage fright and full of jumpin' nerves?"

Lowering her head, Jade murmured, "I felt fine before I got here. But then I saw them sitting down and everything went upside down..."

She could feel Joe staring at her, but Jade was too embarrassed to look at him.

"Well, you seem to be a little better now. Just sit there for another ten minutes or so, until my Clarity can decide if you good to work and take the stage tonight."

"Ugh! Joe, I'm good. I swear!" Jade whined.

Hearing him laugh, Jade finally looked up to see Joe step out of the room, leaving her alone.

***

Jade listened to four songs play over the coffee shop's system before the door to the employee room swung open. Seeing Clarity walk through, Jade straightened up in her chair and held out the empty cup, which got a chuckle out of Clarity.

"Joe told me you chugged it like you were at a house party."

She rolled her eyes while Clarity took a seat next to her. The older woman's eyes worked their way over Jade, taking her in silently. "Yeah, you look better now, but how do you feel here?" Clarity touched the top of Jade's head and smiled.

"I feel...good? Like, yeah, I'm about to take the stage and perform in front of folks that could help me do this professionally, but I'm more excited about the song I get to sing in here tonight." Clarity didn't say anything, so Jade went on to explain, "I was more worried about being sent home and not sharing this new song than I was about not performing in front of the folks from Guerilla Records. Is that bad?"

Clarity took Jade's hands into hers and looked down. When she looked up, Jade felt like she was staring into granny Gladys' eyes. The moment was brief, but it left her speechless.

"No, that ain't wrong at all. I see why my Joe is so full of awe when it comes to you."

The room was silent until Clarity spoke, "You really are coming into your own, baby girl. It's something to behold."

With nowhere to hide from Clarity's praise, Jade lowered her head as a grin broke out across her face. Feeling a hand on top of her head,

Jade looked up and found Clarity staring at her. Through her eyes shone with unshed tears.

"You are full of talent, and folks are drawn to that. But not everyone drawn into your space should have access to it, Jade. Remember that."

Not sure what to say, Jade nodded and Clarity chuckled.

"What I'm saying now may not make all that much sense now, but someday it will. I promise."

Jade sent a smile to Clarity.

"I think I understand. At least a little."

The two laughed before Clarity reached out to cup one of Jade's cheeks.

"Okay, I'll take that for now." The older woman looked at Jade over one more time. "If you agree to stay back here and rest before taking the stage, I won't ask Joe to take you home. Deal?"

When Jade stuck out her hand, Clarity's laughter filled the room.

***

Ten minutes before open mic started, Jade was pacing the small employee room space. She'd already taken out Luxe and ran through the chords she selected for her new song, and waiting to perform it for everyone left Jade feeling like a live wire.

Come on Joe! Let me outta purgatory already!

As soon as the thought left her mind, the door opened and Jade grinned as Joe entered the room. "Look at you! You's ready, uh?"

Jade nodded as she raced to the door and grinned.

"Well, don't let me hold ya back. Come on out and let's get to the stage then."

When they stepped out of the room, Jade looked out at the coffee shop and savored the feeling. Everything, from the tea lights, chatter from the tables throughout the shop, even the sounds of drinks being made at the barista station, they all welcomed her and Jade's nervousness became a thing of the past by the time she got to the stage. Before walking up the short steps, she glanced out at the crowd and found Nashone's eyes on her. He didn't smile right away, but when she sent one his way, Jade watched a grin spread across his face.

"Y'all, welcome my baby girl to the stage - Jade Thornton!"

As the crowd clapped and snapped their fingers, Jade beamed at Joe and he looked at her while speaking again into the mic. "I heard she's giving us another original song tonight, and can't wait to hear it!"

With Luxe to her back, Jade used the strap that was connected to her guitar to bring the guitar to the front of her chest. Joe touched her shoulder on his way off the stage and Jade mouthed 'thank you' to him before speaking into the mic.

"How's everybody doing tonight?" Hearing a few people clap, Jade continued, "So, like Joe said, I got another original for y'all. Hope you like it. But, just in case you don't, please remember the house rules."

That got a few laughs from the crowd and Jade squinted past the house lights to where she saw Nashone standing earlier.

"I'll follow it up with the covers y'all have come to love, but before I start, I wanted to send a special thanks to...to an old friend."

Images appeared in Jade's mind like snapshots of her time with Nashone - from high school to that evening downtown. Each one more live and in color than the last.

"Thank you for coming back into my life and setting things right. I hope you know how much it means to have you by my side again."

Jade tuned out the whispers around her and got her fingers in position on her guitar. Playing in B flat minor was always a challenge for her, but it was the first chord that came to mind for the song she titled, *Sincerely*.

"*In your arms, I feel free...and hope you do too. With my heart now yours, I give you me - sincerely...*"

Lightly plucking at the E flat chord and B 7 chords, one after the other between the chorus, Jade almost forgot to strum the F chord as she went into the bridge of the song. Without the added chord, she was afraid that the more sultry and downtempo song would come across too melancholy. But Jade could hear the rhythmic claps and stomps from the crowd as she made the switch back to B flat minor, and she felt the smile form on her face as she ranged out the last lyric of the song, *"I am sincerely...ready...sincerely."*

When the last note ranged out, the crowd cheered and Jade knew she was cheesin' on stage. But she didn't care.

Joe was right - it does feel good when the crowd connects with you.

"Thanks y'all." was all Jade could get out. She immediately went into one of the cover songs, as promised. When it ended, she blended the chords by playing only the notes and transitioned into the last cover for the night.

At the end of the third song, Jade was afraid to speak. She blinked back happy tears as she turned Luxe around and brought her hands together, bowing in front of the crowd. Looking off at the far end of the stage, Jade saw Clarity and Joe both waiting for her, clapping and cheering louder than everyone else.

***

With her arms linked in Clarity and Joe's, the trio walked away from the stage and Nashone stood in front of them. There were four people behind him, two men, one wearing a suit similar to what Nashone wore his first time in Clarity's. And two women, both wearing leather pants that cling to their slim waists and exposed chests. Only a sheer crop top and a flowy halter top kept them within the coffee shop's dress code. Nashone offered her a small smile when he closed the distance between them a little more. She watched as his head turned slightly to his left and Nashone's eyes hardened before he smiled at them. "Jade! You really did your thing tonight."

Feeling the release of Clarity and Joe's arms, Jade stepped closer to Nashone. "Thanks."

He then gestured to the guy in the suit first and spoke, "This is Erik Sharpe, the founder of Guerilla Records. And the director of A&R, Jon Morae."

Both men reached out to shake Jade's hand. The first one, the guy in the suit, gripped her hand so tight that Jade almost snatched it away when he finally started to let go. "I-it's nice to meet y'all."

"Yeah, thanks for coming out to hear our baby girl take the stage."

Jade grinned at hearing Joe speak about her, but it was short-lived as the founder of Guerilla Records asked, with a voice so deep it sounded like he emerged from the darkest part of a jungle, "Baby girl?"

She almost got lost in the smoothness of his lower octave, until Joe spoke again. "Not blood related, but still our baby girl all the same."

"Awww! That's so...so sweet."

Jade looked at the woman in the crop top after she spoke. The other woman quickly added, "Y'all are just - one BIG family here, uh?"

As the two women giggled, Jade felt her confidence waver. Until she saw Nashone cut his eyes at the two women and then back to her. When he winked, she bit back a laugh. "Something funny, baby girl?" the one in the crop top asked.

Jade smiled, looking at the women and then back to Clarity and Joe. "I never thought about the endearment that much, but to someone who has never been endearing to anything, other than a mirror, it would come off as strange, I guess."

Hearing a snort, Jade looked up to find Jon hiding a smile behind his hand.

"Jade, meet Neequil and Blaze, two of the newest artists to Guerilla Records." Nashone said, extending his hand toward them.

Neither of the women extended a hand out, and Jade kept her face neutral as she addressed them, "Neequil and Blaze? I'm sure you live up to the hype your names give off."

The man in the suit chose to speak then, stepping in front of the women, "I see why Nashone talks so much about you. But as the head brotha in charge - the decision to hire you is mine."

Jade felt soft hands touching her arm, and she noticed Clarity stand closer to her as Erik looked over to Jon. "You A&R, so tell me, is she good?"

While Erik stared at Jade, Nashone came over to her side. Looking up at her, Nashone sent a small smile her way.

"Jon, you know she's more than good! Like I said at -"

Waving a hand in the air, Erik narrowed his eyes onto Nashone, "You speak for Jon now?"

"N-nah."

"Then fall back, rookie."

This guy ain't no joke. Jade thought, as she watched Nashone out of the corner of her eye. She'd never seen him be talked to like that before, and for a second, she worried if he would say something else and make this Erik guy mad. But when he instead put his hands into his pockets and looked at Jon, Jade glanced over at Clarity and Joe.

Seeing their stoic expressions, she listened as Jon answered Erik.

"She is. But I wonder if that's because we're at her home turf. Definitely good with the guitar, and if that song really is an original, she might prove to be a good asset for us."

One of the women scoffed, and Jon added, "Fo sho going to be a time to get settled in when it comes to working with our other talent, but other than that, she's good."

The house music could be heard in the coffee shop as they all watched Erik bring his hand to his chin and turn to Jade. "Why you think I should take a chance and hire you?"

Jade blinked. She didn't think that they would ask her any questions tonight, just come see her play and bounce.

Say something girl! Fore they roll out.

She looked over at Nashone and felt both Joe and Clarity's hands on each of her arms before clearing her throat. "I don't know."

Erik let out a laugh as the women behind him stared hard at her. Nashone brought his head down to her ear and whispered, "Jade - what you doing right now?"

Stepping away from them, Jade kept her eyes on Erik and clasped her shaking hands together before placing them flat to her sides.

"All I know is that I want to play and have my songs heard. And when Nashone said your label was looking for a songwriter, I wanted a chance to try and make that happen with Guerilla Records. But like you said, the decision to hire me ain't mine to make."

When Erik grinned down at Jade, she lowered her eyes and felt Nashone pull her back.

"You got a mouth on you shawty, that's fo sho."

Erik Sharpe wore a suit, similar to one Nashone wore when he first showed up to Clarity's. But they were definitely cut from different cloths, as Nashone's look invited folks to take a closer look and Erik's was all about keeping people away. At least that's what Jade thought while trying to not squirm under his gaze. He was a foot taller than her, and with the dim tea lights accenting Erik's deep reddish hues, she felt her throat constrict under the weight of his presence.

Turning away from her, Jade watched Erik stroll over to Jon and say something to him that she couldn't hear, before walking over to the two women and ushering them to the exit.

"I gotta go introduce the next performer, baby girl."

Hearing Joe's warm voice caused Jade to face him, sending him a wide smile. "Okay."

"Mariah looks busy behind the counter." Clarity said.

Jade looked at both of them and nodded, saying, "I'll be there to help behind the counter soon, boss."

Clarity laughed as she leaned forward and kissed Jade on the cheek. "You did good tonight."

Watching them walk in opposite directions, Jade looked back at the stage.

I still can't believe they came out to hear me! Maybe they really do wanna work with me.

"You were better than good up there tonight, Jade."

She turned to see Nashone staring at her, and Jade had to remind herself to breathe as Nashone's eyes twinkled on her under the tealights above. His brown skin seemed to glow against the lights, and Jade found herself stealing glances up at his faint pink lips.

"Thanks."

Joe's booming voice crackled over the mic as he introduced the crowd to the next artist, and Jade looked behind Nashone to see Erik making his way back toward them.

"Good to see you taking your job seriously, rookie. She got talent."

Overhearing Erik talk about her, Jade could feel the hope rising in her chest.

"But I ain't gonna make no decision right on the spot." Jade's nervousness took a dive to the pit of her stomach and came to a stop at Erik's words until he added, "Since she's ya girl, I'll send you back here to tell her what I decided tomorrow. Let's roll out."

She watched as Nashone followed Erik out of the coffee shop, but before Nashone opened the door for Erik, he turned back to Jade and sent another smile in her direction.

Chapter Ten
Grimy Graces

The next day, Jade could hardly sit still. With Diamond and her nephew away visiting his grandparents, she chose to spend the day at home with Xavier before working that afternoon. They were on the couch, sharing a bag of chips, and watching *Final Destination*. But Jade couldn't say what was happening on the screen. When Xavier laughed, she jumped.

"Jade? You okay?" he asked.

She tried to act like everything was good when she shrugged and reached for the bag between them, but Xavier snatched it away.

"Nah, you buggin' about Guerilla Records, right?"

"No."

Even she didn't believe the word as it made its way out of her mouth. Feeling Xavier's stare, Jade tried again, "No?"

"Do I need to call Raquel over so we can get you straight?"

The thought of her two friends tag teaming her with affirmations and probably drinking while doing it made Jade giggle.

I wish I had time today to just chill with them, but I gotta go to Clarity's.

Thinking of a way to get Xavier's mind off calling for reinforcements, Jade took the bowl of chips from him and lit up when the perfect distraction came to mind. "I see you ain't rocking your boot no more. Does that mean you still on lockdown or nah?"

Xavier side eyed Jade before picking up a chip and flicking it in her direction. "Since you must know, I've been given permission to go out for trips that take no longer than 30 to 45 minutes."

Jade mimicked his side eye and stood from the couch. While walking toward her room she said playfully, "Well, if you wouldn't mind giving me a ride to Clarity's, maybe Nashone would be there and..."

She could hear Xavier struggling to get up from the couch before turning around and finding her friend covered in chips. Laughing, Jade went to help him clean up the mess and confirmed, "So, you'll drive me to Clarity's then?"

"Hell yeah! I'll get my keys now." Xavier said.

Jade grinned while watching Xavier wobble and hop to the other side of the living room, managing not to fall as he scooped up his car keys from the end table.

"Okay, let me grab your crutches."

***

Just as Jade was opening the passenger side door to Xavier's ride, she heard him whisper loudly, "Damn! Who's the hottie over there?"

"You would spend your first free minutes outside chasing tail."

"But Jade! He is a good looking piece of ass."

She laughed as Xavier scoffed, "Shame too, don't think he plays for my team."

With Xavier now standing in front of her, Jade started to hand him one of the crutches before hearing someone call out her name. Turning around, Jade tried to keep the corners of her lips from turning upward at the sight of Nashone walking toward them.

"Hey Jade. I didn't know when your shift started, guess I was too early."

Xavier leaned close to Jade's ear and whispered, "THAT's Nashone?" When Jade nodded, he laughed. "Some girls have all the fun."

Keeping her eyes on Nashone, Jade rubbed her hands on the front of her denim shorts before answering. "Yeah. Um, today's my half day, so I was hanging out with a friend."

She watched as Nashone looked behind her and flatly asked, "A friend?"Xavier let out a snort and before Jade could say more, he spoke, "Yeah, I'm her good friend, Xavier. But I'd *love* to become close friends with *you*."

Seeing Nashone take in Xavier's baggy jeans and white crop top fit, Jade tried not to laugh when he coughed.

"Um, yeah. I'm good." He looked at Jade, and the half smile he sent her way left her throat dry. "Can we talk right quick?"

She nodded and they walked inside Clarity's. Feeling the gush of wind from Nashone opening the door, Jade closed her eyes and let Xavier hop in before her.

What if Erik sent him to tell me no? What if he says yes and wants me to work with Guerilla Records after all?

Jade waved at Clarity and Joe, as they sat at the table closest to the stage. Pulling out a chair for her, Xavier waited for her to sit before doing the same. "So, you two known each other for a while?"

Hearing Nashone's voice broke Jade out of her thoughts. She looked between the two and answered. "Yeah."

Xavier laughed. "Me and Jade been friends since her senior year of high school. Guess that was after you already bounced though."

She watched Nashone shift in his seat, cutting his eyes from Xavier to Jade. "Oh. That's cool."

With Jade's nerves racing in her veins, she blurted out, "So, what did Erik say? Does he wanna hire me?"

Nashone sighed and Jade started to prepare herself for the worst. Straightening her shoulders, she let out a shaky laugh. "Well, you didn't promise me the gig, so we all good."

"The man ain't said nothing yet Jade, so stop trying to end things before they start." Xavier said. He then reached out to place a hand on hers and added, "Just let him speak."

They both looked over at Nashone, while he kept his stare on Jade. "This morning, Erik called me into his office and ... he wants to offer you the job."

Grabbing Xavier's hand, Jade watched as Nashone sighed. "But Erik says before he does, he wants everyone you'd be working with to hear you perform."

Jade saw Xavier's face scrunch up before he said slowly, "What? Like a private show?"

Nashone nodded, and Xavier chimed in with a question of his own, "Where?"

"Jon suggested at the Guerilla Records sound room, and Erik agreed. They sent me to see if you can be there and perform next week."

Why doesn't Nashone look happy? This was his plan from the beginning, right?

She tried not to notice how Nashone's usually light and charming smile all but went away. In its place was a small one that didn't reach his eyes. Even the way he sat was weird, like it hurt too much to move. He was almost as still as stone sitting across from them, and something about it made Jade uneasy. She didn't get a chance to think any more about it when she heard Nashone ask her, "Jade, I know this is what we planned, but you don't have to do it. I...I'll understand if you ain't down to perform outside of Clarity's."

Jade didn't hesitate as the words left her mouth, "Yeah. Tell me when and I'll be there."

"Oh shit! You're gonna do Jade?" Xavier asked.

When she looked at him, Jade could feel the excitement bursting to come out of her as she nodded quickly.

"That's what's up! Go show them why you're the next songwriter for their team!"

The more Xavier spoke, the quieter Nashone seemed, pulling Jade out of the moment. Her glance landed on Nashone's and she caught him looking down at his phone, a light crease forming between his eyes.

When he looked back at Jade, he let out a sigh. "Are you sure? You don't need time to think about it?"

"What else is there to think about, Nashone? This is what they wanted to happen, so why put it off?"

Does he think I can't do it?

Yeah, Jade has only been performing again a little over two months now, and each set has been at Clarity's. But for some reason, the thought of Nashone doubting that she was ready left a bitter taste in her mouth.

"Do you think I can't perform outside of Clarity's?"

Jade heard footsteps from behind her but kept her sights on Nashone as he leaned forward and sighed before sitting back straight.

"I just want to make sure you're okay, Jade. That's all."

The two stared into each other's eyes, until Joe's voice rang out, "He's just looking out for you, baby girl."

Nashone broke their stare and locked eyes with Joe. The two then looked back toward Jade with downcast eyes, and the excitement Jade felt before was gone.

I have to do this - I'm tired of people always doubting me.

"Well, I don't need him looking out for me!" Bawling up her fist, Jade glared at Nashone and barked, "When I needed you to be there for me, you bounced. So just do your job and tell me when I need to be at Guerilla Records."

"Jade! Girl..." Xavier whispered.

Clarity and Joe looked at Jade and Nashone, as Nashone stood up. Pushing in the chair, he avoided Jade's stare before saying over his shoulder, "They wanna see you at the sound room next Friday night."

Everyone watched as Nashone walked out of the coffee shop, almost bumping into Mariah on her way inside. She jumped back and let him pass before asking out loud, "Dang, who pissed him off?"

"Jade, I know it's none of my business, but..." Xavier started, only to be cut off by Jade.

"You was right the first time - it's not your business. So don't say nothin."

Joe walked in front of Jade, but it was Clarity who spoke, "Baby girl, that boy seems to be struggling with something. Maybe it has something to do with whatever happened between you two in the past, or something with this record company that he can't talk about."

Jade opened her mouth to speak, but Joe shook his head and Clarity continued, "Whatever it is, you need to apologize. Or I'll put you on the schedule for Friday, and you will have to choose."

The threat hung in the air and Jade looked down at her hands as she tried not to let her anger show.

This ain't right! What I got to say sorry for?

Jade looked at Clarity and asked, "You'd make me choose between the showcase or working here?"

When Clarity didn't answer, Jade jumped out of her seat, shaking the table. "That's some bullshit!"

"You watch your mouth!" Joe bellowed.

The coffee shop was silent as Jade stared at Joe and Clarity.

"Let me just head out right quick..."

Xavier reached out and grabbed his car keys and crutches from the table. Though before he reached the front door, Xavier turned around and looked at Jade, "I've known you for a minute now mana, and I've never heard you raise your voice. Not even when I ate the last of your gummy bear stash before finals last year. Whatever's on your mind right now..."

Jade bit her lip and Xavier paused. He looked over at Joe and Clarity before speaking to her again. "I'll see you at home later."

With Xavier gone, Jade had no choice but to face Clarity and Joe. Neither of them looked happy so Jade made sure to choose her next words carefully. "I know I was a little out-of-pocket-"

"Just a little?" Clarity interjected, her stare hard on Jade.

She took a deep breath and let it out slowly as she went on, "But I'm tired of being treated like I don't know what I'm doing. Yeah, okay, I was bugging before my last performance. And I probably shouldn't have started shouting earlier. But I got this!"

Joe opened his mouth to speak and Jade rushed out, "I'm ready to try - to put myself out there. But y'all acting like I can't do that and it really...that hurts more than being made fun of."

Jade fought the stinging sensation behind her eyes as she started to walk away. Joe blocked her path and she tried to go around him only for him to side step her.

"Baby girl..."

Hearing the softness return to his voice, Jade peeked up and saw him looking over at Clarity. Knowing that no matter what, Clarity meant what she said about having Jade chose. So she turned to look at Clarity and told her, "I'll call Nashone tonight and apologize. May I please have next Friday off?"

Clarity walked over to Jade. She waited until Jade met her stare before speaking, "I'll let you know after your shift ends. And after you've called that boy."

It took all Jade's self control to not show her disapproval with that answer, but she kept her face neutral when she spoke again.

"Okay."

***

She had all night to think about the perfect apology to give Nashone over the phone, but when her shift ended, Jade forgot everything she wanted to say. Her hands were damp as she pushed the buttons on her Nokia phone and put it to her ear.

What if he doesn't answer? What will I tell Clarity?

Jade didn't have to think long about the growing list of 'what ifs' once she heard Nashone answer the line. "What's up?"

Instead of answering right away, Jade glanced around the break room and sighed while looking up toward the big black and white clock that hung above a photo of Clarity and Joe. They weren't physically in the room but somehow the photo of them smiling down at her made it feel like they were. Clearing her throat, Jade finally spoke, "Um, hey. I was calling cause...I, um...I'm sorry."

Nashone said nothing after her apology, so Jade tried again, "Hey, did you hear me?"

"Yeah, I heard you."

The phone started to feel like a cinderblock in her hand as Jade went on, "So why you ain't saying nothing?"

"What you want me to say Jade?"

Why he gotta make this harder than it already is?

She almost swore she saw the photo above the clock move. Her heartbeat picked up speed when she heard footsteps coming closer to the break room, so Jade thought fast.

"I ain't mean to yell at you earlier, but you asking me if I was sure really felt like you ain't think I could do this. And if you thought that I couldn't - why did you ask me to try to begin with?"

Jade heard the house music inside the coffee shop stop playing while she waited for Nashone to speak. "Jade, I been knew you could play. But I remember how you acted back in the day when I found your songbook." He paused and Jade could hear a faint bass line in the background before Nashone continued. "I know you heard about Guerilla Records, but...I promise you, whatever you heard ain't nowhere near the truth. It- it's different working for them than doing your own thing."

She let Nashone's words settle into her thoughts, and tried to find the right ones of her own.

Maybe Joe was right - sounds like Nashone was just trying to look after me.

Though even after hearing him out, Jade had to know for sure. Taking a deep breath, she closed her eyes and gripped the phone.

"You said you remember how I was when you found my songbook that one time, and that's why you wanted to be sure I was really down to do this. What if...what if I let you read it?"

"What?"

"My songbook. What if I let you read it before my performance? Then you can not only see that I'm ready, but be able to tell me how the artists will respond to some of the lyrics I have in mind."

Nashone's voice was muffled for a minute while Jade waited for his answer. Hearing a loud creaking sound, Jade's eyes darted to the break room's entrance and she watched as Clarity marched inside and stood beside her.

"Yeah, cool, okay. I can do that."

Jade bit down on her lip when she asked, "You free tomorrow? I'm off."

"Yeah. Where you wanna meet?"

Not wanting eyes on them at Clarity's, Jade blurted out the first place that came to mind, "SoundTracks. Let's meet there."

It had been months since she'd been to her first job, but Jade still loved SoundTracks. The guy working behind the counter noticed her when she stepped past the security panels and sent Jade a head nod, which she returned. On the speakers, she heard the end of a Dirty South inspired song and briefly wondered if her old boss was in that day.

Walking to the New Releases section, Jade adjusted the strap to her messenger bag, bringing it closer to her side while taking her time surveying the different vinyl and CD's that were on display. There seemed to be more vinyl on the shelf, and she was left wondering if the old school sound was taking over again.

"Guess vinyl really is doing the damn thing."

Hearing Nashone's voice behind her, Jade reminded herself to stay calm when she turned to face it. Seeing him dressed in a pair of baggy denim jeans and a crisp yellow t-shirt, she matched his grin with her own.

"To be fair, it never really left."

He picked up a vinyl album close to her face, and Jade closed her eyes as memories of what she last envisioned about those fingers and hands came back to her mind. Remembering that SoundTracks was the place where they had first met, Jade avoided Nashone's stare. Her face grew warm while she thought back to that day.

What do I say now?

"I ain't give Guerilla Records an answer yet about you being there on Friday."

Jade's eyes landed on his and she breathed in and out quickly before asking, "Why not?"

"I wanted to give you more time to really think about it."

Their eyes stayed on one another, until another song began to play over the store's speakers. It was Nashone that looked away first, clearing his throat.

"So, you finally gonna let me look at your songbook?"

I still can't believe I agreed to this...

Reaching for the strap to her bag, Jade let out a small sigh and scrunched up her nose when Nashone laughed. She stepped forward and Nashone quickly brought his hands out to his chest while shaking his head. "I see you still protective 'bout your little book." Just as she opened her mouth to speak, Nashone continued, "I'm just saying. This was your idea, so if you gonna be mad with anybody, best start with yourself."

Not ready to admit that he was right, Jade raised her chin and asked with as much false annoyance as she could muster.

"Since you know so much, why'd you agree to meet me today then?"

She watched as Nashone turned his head away from her, while bringing one of his hands to the back of his head. When he slowly rounded back to her and grinned, Jade swore her heart stopped for a second. Titling his head to Jade's messenger bag and then up to her stare, Nashone smoothed tenor voice was low when he answered.

"I dunno. Guess I just wanted to see you again."

Jade. Jade! Girl, focus!

Blinking herself out of the haze she was falling under in Nashone's presence, Jade swallowed hard. "Well, I ain't just gonna open it up for you here."

Nashone's eyes widened before a smirk appeared on his face. "So...where you wanna go?"

When Jade didn't answer, Nashone let out a low chuckle and brought his eyes back to her. He looked at her like he knew something that she didn't, and it bugged Jade.

"What?" she finally asked.

Nashone took his time glancing down, and then back up to Jade's face again before drawling out, "Nothing."

Jade felt her stomach clench, prompting her to ask another question. "Are you hungry?"

***

The 239 Diner was busier than Jade thought it would be, but she didn't mind. Nashone held the door to the diner open for her, and Jade caught a whiff of his cologne. Smiling at the familiar scent, it reminded her of their days together in the practice room back in high school.

Never thought I'd ever wanna go back to NLH, but now I kinda wish we could.

"Gone and take a seat, we'll be right with y'all." The server instructed.

She watched Nashone send a head nod to the server before leading them to a booth in the middle of the diner. He waited for Jade to slide inside before sitting next to her. "Why you ain't sit on the other side?"

When he leaned in closer, Jade jerked her head back, bumping it against the wall. She wanted to disappear as Nashone didn't try to hide his laughter. Once he stopped, Jade rolled her eyes at him and sighed. He briefly closed his eyes when she did, and Jade noticed his chest rise and slowly fall before he opened his eyes again.

"Figured it'd be better to see what you have in your songbook. You know, by sitting on the same side as you."

The small clenching in Jade's stomach from earlier came back, but this time it felt stronger. And as her eyes lowered to Nashone's lips, the feeling traveled lower, causing Jade to quickly sit up straight. "Oh."

"Y'all ready to order?"

Hearing the server address them, Jade blurted out. "Fries!"

She then directed her attention to their server and watched them write on a small pad.

Before he spoke, Nashone glanced over her way and Jade felt like she was laying right under a heat lamp. "Two order of fries and two lemonades, please."

Once the server scribbled the order on their notepad, they looked at the two of them and added, "Anything else?"

Nashone turned to face Jade again, this time glancing down at her lips as he asked, "You want something else?"

What's wrong with me?

Biting the inside of her lip to try and control the feeling that was now traveling from Jade's stomach up to her chest. The feeling then ziplined, making its way even lower, and Jade didn't trust what sounds she'd make if she opened her mouth to answer him. Shaking her head, Jade hoped Nashone wouldn't ask her any more questions.

"Can you add a basket of chicken fingers too, please?"

When the server nodded, Nashone scooted over a little and Jade released a breath she forgot she was holding.

"Thank you."

With their server gone, Jade kept her hands tightly on the strap of her messenger bag. Staring hard at Nashone, she touched the top of the flap and unbuttoned it, flipping it over to take out her green composition book. Nashone didn't say anything when he placed his hands out to accept the book, but instead smiled at Jade. She cut her eyes away from his and mumbled out, "Joe's read a few of the lyrics that I tabbed. He thinks they might be good warm-ups for introducing Guerilla Records to my style."

Nashone quietly read through several of the marked pages, slowly nodding before closing the book. When he returned the book, their hands touched and her eyes widened. That touch summoned a spark throughout Jade's body, and she wondered if Nashone noticed too. If he did, he didn't say so. Instead, he held her stare as he said, " I knew it."

Taken aback, Jade asked, "Knew what?"

"I knew your songs would be hella good."

Jade's mouth fell open as the warmth she felt in the pit of her stomach made it below her waist. Her breathing felt labored as she looked Nashone in the eye, and he grinned. "Thank you for finally sharing your songs with me."

She didn't get a chance to say anything, as their order arrived then, and Jade grabbed her lemonade with both hands. Not bothering to use the plastic straw that was placed in front of her, Jade welcomed the sweet yet tart cool drink while taking several hearty gulps before placing the cup back on the table with shaking hands.

"You want me to bring you another one, sweetie?"

Jade nodded to their server and avoided Nashone's smirk as she reached for a chicken finger. It didn't take long for them to finish their meal, and when Nashone paid the bill, Jade looked at him as he walked them to 239 diner exit and took a few mints from a large bowl next to the to-go counter.

"Um, can we..." she muttered while looking down at her feet.

When Nashone turned to face her, Jade's throat went dry.

"What?"

Not wanting to leave him just yet, Jade forced herself to quickly look up just as Nashone started to lean down to hear what she was trying to say. Her eyes widened and she tried to back away, but before she could utter a word they collided into one another.

"Oh shit!" Nashone said, rubbing his forehead with his hand.

Jade felt the blush travel all over her face as she squeaked out, "I-I'm sorry. I was..."

Standing this close to Nashone, the words Jade wanted to say all but disappeared. The wind picked up around them, with a gentle breeze caressing their faces. She watched as Nashone briefly closed his eyes and noted that his lashes looked just as soft as they did years ago. Jade reached out a hand to lightly touch them to find out for herself, while also sweeping a finger across one of Nashone's thick eyebrows.

"Ayee...what you doing?" he asked with a chuckle.

I don't know...but I don't want to stop.

Jade's pulse was racing as she stared into Nashone's hazel eyes.

"Just...um, can we go somewhere?" She knew she wasn't making much sense, and Nashone's raised eyebrow confirmed it. Steadying her breath with a few short inhales and quick exhales, Jade tried again. "I mean, if you ain't busy, can we go downtown?"

Stepping back, Nashone maintained Jade's stare. "Oh. Umm, yeah, that's cool."

The drive downtown was quick and Jade immediately hopped out of Nashone's ride when he parked. Going to the meter, she put in all the coins she had in her pocket. It was enough to cover the parking spot for three hours.

"Now we here, what do you wanna do?"

Jade turned to find Nashone walking toward her. Each step seemed to match her heartbeat, and by the time he reached her side, Jade had to ball up her fist to keep from taking his hand.

"I don't know. Can we walk around?"

When he nodded, Jade released a sigh and the two began walking side by side on the sidewalk. A block ahead, she noticed someone setting up to play. They were not much younger than her and Nashone. The kid took their time getting their case and sign just the way they wanted before turning to pick up their instrument - a viola.

Breaking the silence, Nashone pointed in the kid's direction. "Wanna go check them out?"

"Yeah, let's go hear 'em."

As they listened to the kid warm up with a quick scale check, Nashone asked Jade, "When was the last time you came out here? To play?"

"It's been a minute." Jade answered. "Not since my senior year."

Notes ranged out from the performer's viola seconds later. The piece they played sounded like a melody for two and Jade's palms grew sweaty from the thought. Rubbing her hands along the side of her jeans, she remembered the bills she had and reached inside. Pulling out a few singles, she stepped closer to toss them into the instrument case. Nashone stopped her when he covered her hand with his, sending Jade's heart sailing up to her throat.

"I got it." he said softly.

Jade looked on while Nashone peeled a few ones from his wallet and placed them into the kid's instrument case. While playing, the kid looked up at them and smiled widely, picking up the pace of the piece he played. Now that he had an audience, he lowered his waist as he strung the viola, causing it to repeat for a few more seconds before the echoes changed into a familiar R&B sound.

"He fo sho did not study that one in school." Nashone said, and Jade let out a giggle.

When she put her money away, Nashone took her hand into his. Looking at him, Jade said nothing as he led them away from the performer and the crowd. Off in the distance the sun was nearing the end of its set, showing bright yet rich hues of oranges, pinks, and purples that hinted at the upcoming evening sky. Feeling Nashone's hand still in hers, Jade looked up as he stopped walking and she closed her eyes. Leaning against his chest, Jade listened to the faint sounds of the street performers behind them as the strong steady beating of Nashone's heart thrummed in her ear.

"You good?" she heard Nashone ask out loud.

Instead of answering him, Jade brought her head up and looked him in the eye. She watched his stare drift to her lips and that feeling from earlier returned in full force when Nashone's tongue swiped quickly over his bottom lip.

"Jade..."

She tilted her head and moved closer, almost blindly toward Nashone's lips. When she felt their softness against hers, the butterflies fluttered wildly around in her stomach while Nashone's hand freed hers to bring her even closer into his warmth. Time didn't stop, but instead got lost as Jade's lips introduced themselves to Nashone's. She brought her hands up to his face. Their lips met softly at first, until Nashone's head leaned forward and Jade followed with a sound she'd never heard before.

It was short, but full of excitement, and Nashone wasted no time responding, as his tongue lightly touched Jade's lip. When she gasped, her mouth opened, allowing their silent conversation to go deeper. The scent of spearmint reached Jade's nose, and though she was unsure of what would happen next, Jade eventually brushed the tip of her tongue to Nashone's. His arms tightened around her briefly before he pulled away. Slowly opening her eyes, Jade looked up and saw Nashone watching her.

"I always wondered...what that would feel like," she whispered. Nashone said nothing, so Jade focused on her breathing before asking, "Was it good?"

His eyes widened before she felt Nashone's forehead rest against hers. "You playin' me right now?"

"No. I-I ain't got nothing to compare it to." Jade kept her eyes on his chest as she rushed out. "Since it's the first time, I, uh..."

Feeling Nashone's fingertips touch her chin, Jade closed her eyes as he brought her face up to meet his.

"Jade. Look at me."

The deep whispered request left her unable to ignore him, and she sighed while opening her eyes. "Are you saying what I think you saying?"

When she nodded, Nashone turned his head and quickly brought it back toward her. This time when their lips touched, Jade struggled to keep up. Nashone didn't ask for permission as his tongue sought out hers. Her whole body vibrated as his moan connected them. The hands that Jade had begun to think about daily since they last spoke alone at Clarity's roamed along her back, freely making their way down to the middle, stopping just before her ass. And she wanted them to continue to get to know every inch of her. Before thoughts of telling Nashone as much left her mouth, Jade's lips parted from Nashone's. They both stood in front of each other, trying to catch their breath.

"Jade..."

With her body now warm all over and ready to keep talking without words to his, Jade answered breathlessly, "Yeah?"

"I don't want you to do the private showcase."

Blinking her eyes, Jade glanced into Nashone's.

"I know this was my idea, and I ain't got no right to ask you this...but I'mma do it anyway. Please don't come to the showcase at Guerilla next week."

Completely confused, Jade managed to ask him, "W-why do you not want me to do the showcase?"

Nashone stepped away from Jade, and she watched as he paced the small space in front of her. He looked over at her and Jade could see his chest rise and fall for a few beats before he started to walk back to her and stopped, leaving a few feet between them. His lips were in a tight line until he spoke.

"I...just don't think it's the right move. Erik is - he's..." His words fell flat before Nashone tried again. "If you give me time, I'm sure I can coordinate with the rest of the record company - even some of the other artists - about a bigger showcase. One we can have at Clarity's instead."

Jade wasn't sure if Nashone was talking to her anymore, as she watched him nod his head and stare off in the opposite direction.

"Yeah, I can do that."

Nashone finally looked back at Jade and she tried to choose her words carefully. "I think I should stick to the plan."

When she saw his jaw tighten, Jade explained, "It wouldn't look right if I don't show up to this showcase, Nashone. What would everyone say about me then?" He started to speak, but Jade held up a hand to stop him. "I don't want to give Guerilla Records time to doubt me and move on to someone else. And wouldn't it look bad on you too? You just started working in this position - I would feel awful if me not showing up put you at risk of losing your job."

"Jade..."

Nashone ran his hands along the top of his head. The stare he sent Jade's way left her unable to move.

"If it came down to it, I'd fo sho bounce instead of have you do this showcase."

Her eyes widened as Nashone closed the space between them, "Please, just think about it. And if you decide to go through with it, let me be there when you do perform in front of Erik and them, okay?"

"Okay."

His arms were around her again, and Jade felt each shaky breath he let out. To try and comfort him, she wrapped her arms around his neck and brought Nashone closer. When their foreheads gently touched once more, Jade closed her eyes as Nashone spoke again, his voice barely above a whisper, "Thank you."

Chapter Eleven
Paying Dues

That night, once she got home, Jade thought about what Nashone asked her. After taking a shower and putting on her favorite onesies, Jade paced the living floor, trying to understand why he'd ask her to say no to the private showcase with Guerilla Records. Jade brought her hands up to her lips and paused.

Ugh! I should've asked him to tell me why he don't want me to do it.

The more she thought about it, not doing the showcase just didn't make sense. Sighing, Jade decided to go to bed. Though once in the bathroom, her mind began replaying the kiss she and Nashone shared over and over. Even while brushing her teeth, Jade imagined the feel of Nashone's lips against hers and she found herself not able to look at her reflection in the mirror. The heat crept into her cheeks, causing Jade to turn on the faucet and reach out her hands to scoop cold water into the palms of her hands. Splashing the water that collected into her hands against her face twice, Jade still couldn't shake the memory.

Yeah, so we kissed - it ain't no big deal.

Even as she said the words to herself, Jade couldn't believe them. Now in bed, she snuggled under the comforter and turned off the light on her nightstand. Which only seemed to make the replay of kissing Nashone more clearer in her mind. She tossed, turned, and finally let out a high pitched squeal before being able to fall asleep.

***

Morning came way too early, as Jade squinted her eyes at the bright rays of sun that peeked through the curtains in her bedroom. She stretched when getting out of bed and smiled as she heard the sounds of the radio playing from in the kitchen. Jade tried to tip toe out of her room to the bathroom, but before she reached the door knob, the sounds of the radio disappeared. Turning around, Jade saw Xavier wearing his usual morning attire - a pair of brightly colored briefs and no shirt - while holding a skillet.

"You really thought I wouldn't hear you getting up? Mana, listening to the radio and cooking while waiting for your sleepyhead self to emerge from your room is easy."

"Can I at least pee first?" Jade asked.

Xavier laughed as he turned back to the stove, leaving Jade to go and freshen up for the day. Opening the bathroom door, Jade slowly stuck her head out and snuck a peek at Xavier dancing while flipping a pancake over the store.

Well, at least I'mma eat good while getting grilled.

She didn't make it to their small kitchenette table to sit down before Xavier started his round of twenty questions, "So, why you went off like that the other day?"

Jade looked up at Xavier and poked out her bottom lip. He sighed before taking another clean plate out of the dishrack and flopped two pancakes, a serving of scrambled eggs, along with several turkey sausage links onto before walking toward her. Stopping a few feet from the table, Xavier held the plate away from Jade as she reached out to accept it.

"Being cute will only get you so far. You going to answer my question or nah?"

Accepting that there's no way out of this and not wanting her breakfast to get cold, Jade mumbled, "I don't know."

"Girl, speak up or I'll sit this plate down and start grubbing on it myself."

"Alright! Dang!" Jade stared at the plate in Xavier's hand and sighed. "I was mad."

Xavier took a step closer and Jade inhaled the savory yet sweet smells of breakfast as she went on to explain. "Okay, fine. I was embarrassed. When Nashone asked me in front of y'all if I was sure about performing at Guerilla, it felt like he was saying I couldn't. So I snapped."

She kept her eyes on the plate as Xavier placed it in front of her. When he did, Jade grabbed the fork and butter knife from off the table and started cutting the fluffy pancakes into smaller square pieces. There was a bit of butter melting in the middle, just the way she liked it, and Jade grinned while reaching for the syrup in the middle of the table to drizzle over the warm breakfast cakes.

"Yes you did go off, that's for sure. "

Jade took a bite of the pancakes and let out a groan of delight. "Mmmmh! I've missed your cooking Xavier!"

"Don't you even try to butter me up, Jade. Cause I still have questions."

She continued to eat while Xavier walked back to the counter to turn down the radio. Fixing himself a plate, he sat across from her. Jade felt his stare and wolfed down some more eggs before she got up to get a glass of orange juice. The silence was loud as Jade reached into the cabinet again to get another glass. Xavier's stare followed her every movement as Jade poured the juice into their glasses and sat the drinks onto the table.

"Didn't he approach first? About working with the record company?"

Xavier's question threw Jade for a second, but after she took a sip of orange juice she recovered. "Yeah, he did."

"So why would he all of a sudden doubt that you could do this, Jade? That don't make no sense."

Toying with her last turkey sausage link, Jade answered absentmindedly, "I don't know..."

"Jade, you know we homies, right?"

When Jade nodded, Xavier continued, "But do you think...that maybe - just maybe - when Nashone asked you if you were sure about doing the showcase... that he wasn't the one thinking that you could do this?"

Dropping her fork onto the plate, the clanking noise in the quiet kitchen.

"I-I don't understand wh-"

Xavier looked over directly at her and Jade crossed her legs together as she tried to not look away. "I think you do."

Jade blinked away the feelings that threatened to leave her eyes as Xavier went on, "Did you have a moment where maybe *you* thought you couldn't do it after meeting the peeps from Guerilla Records?"

When Jade didn't answer, Xavier took a sip of his orange juice and she watched as his face softened. "It's okay to be scared sometimes, Jade."

Her throat began to burn when Xavier placed a hand on top of hers. "You weren't there Xavier. Those girls from the label...I didn't say nothin' to Nashone and them, but they..."

The more she tried to get the words to come out of her mouth, the more the burning knot grew. Jade took a deep breath and let the flashbacks from Northern Lights pass by in her mind when she let the breath out. "They reminded me of how the girls in high school made me feel."

Xavier squeezed her hand and Jade asked him a question, "How come? I mean, I thought I was through feeling like I did then. How come they can still make me feel like that?"

"High school never ends for some peeps, Jade. "

She looked across the table at Xavier and saw him blinking away tears of his own. "You know I came out my senior year of high school, right?"

When Jade nodded, Xavier continued, "But before that, everyone seemed to already know I was into guys. No matter what I did to be liked, or fit in, it never worked. So when I was finally ready to come out, I thought 'Yeah, once I do then everything's gonna change.' But the only thing that changed for me back then was my address."

She then took their hands and intertwined them, sniffling. "Weren't you scared?"

"Hell yeah I was scared!"

Laughter filled the otherwise quietness before Xavier explained. "But also, I was really excited. I was lucky to have friends that helped, but I found a job and soon got my own place. Then I met your weird ass."

He playfully rolled his eyes when she went to let go of his hand. But when she did, Xavier gripped it even tighter. "It's okay to be scared, Jade. That way when those old feelings pop up, you can own up to them. And then kick their sorry asses to the curb!"

Jade giggled again.

"High school may not end for some, but you ain't in high school no more mana. And when you take the stage again for them peeps, remember that so you can stunt on them fools."

With her hand still in his, Jade took her other one and enclosed it around them. "Yeah, that's what I'm gonna do."

When she and Xavier finished their breakfast, Jade made sure to volunteer to wash the dishes, which ended up taking longer because Xavier just had to re-teach her how to salsa while they listened to the radio. Every time her wet hands touched his back, Xavier would shimmy and Jade's laughter ranged out over the music. Once the last song ended, Xavier twirled out of Jade's arms and grinned.

"I missed doing silly shit like this with you mana."

Jade looked over at her friend while he made his way out of the kitchen. "Me too."

As he turned the corner, she asked quickly, "How about after I perform for Guerilla Records we have a late night session?" Xavier stopped and looked over at her, prompting Jade to add, "We could make tortas and stay up late watching old telenovelas?"

"We haven't done that since you moved in chicka - I'm down!"

She laughed again when Xavier started doing the washing machine all the way to his room.

***

Once she got to Clarity's for the night shift, Jade was glad she wasn't performing. The barista station was packed, as it was finals week and more students came in to chillax after their exams. She and Mariah were running back and forth, filling orders, making drinks, and bussing tables. With everything going on around her, Jade had completely forgotten about letting Nashone know her decision. Until she managed to take a break and checked her phone. The low smooth jazz music played in the background while she scanned the five messages from him.

Guess I better tell him what's up.

Her message was short, but Nashone responded to it all the same, asking Jade to let him drive her to Guerilla Records.

"Yo Jade! Can you grab some more napkins from the stockroom?"

Mariah's request left her punching 'yes' onto the Nokia phone, before sliding it into the back pocket of her shorts.

"Okay!"

While searching and finally finding the box of napkins, Jade paused as she heard Joe announce a new performer. Memories of her first night at Clarity's came to mind and she leaned against the metal stacks in the storage room and felt a smile spread across her face. Hearing Mariah call out to her snapped Jade out of her thoughts, and she grabbed the box again while making her way out of the room.

The crowd is really feeling this one.

When Jade restocked the counter with napkins, she joined Mariah behind the counter. With everyone finger snapping and bobbing their heads to this new spoken word and keyboardist, the two looked at one another and smiled.

"I like their flow." Jade said, following into step with the major scales that danced along to the poetry that came out over the mic.

Mariah looked over at her and then back to the stage. "I like his fit."

Hearing this, Jade had to put a hand over her mouth to hide a laugh. "Seriously?"

"What? Can't a brotha be poetic and fione?"

Jade let out a small laugh and surveyed the coffeeshop. Seeing Clarity walk over to the station, she bumped her hip into Mariah's and tilted her head in the direction Clarity was coming from.

"We better look busy, 'fore boss lady find something for us to do."

"Whatever, you know Clarity be enjoying the vibes too."

Proving her point, Mariah stayed still when Clarity reached the counter. She and Clarity shared a smile before the older woman looked down at the desserts in the window and ran a hand over the countertop. Her finger paused over the pecan pie before she looked up at the two of them.

"I got it." Jade said as she went to retrieve a small plate and fork.

The keyboardist ended their set and the crowd sent them a thunderous applause. Jade looked out at the scene and smiled while cutting Clarity a slice of the pie.

"He's good."

Soon her eyes landed on Jade's when the pecan pie was placed in front of her. Jade looked on as she dug a fork in and brought it to her mouth. "Maybe y'all can try to duet together sometime?"

"Me?" Jade asked.

Clarity's laughter danced over the chatter in the coffee shop. "Yeah, you. Ain't that's what you'll be doing at Guerilla Records?"

Jade hadn't thought about that. Her confusion must have shown, as Clarity asked, "What? You just gonna perform your songs the way you want and hope they like it?"

"I..I don't know."

She looked down at the dessert counter and thought about what exactly it was that she'd be signing to do at the record company.

I mean, I have songs and would like to write more with some artists, I guess, but I didn't think how that would go down.

"Well, you might want to know what it is you want to do, if Guerilla Records does hire you, baby girl."

Jade slowly met Clarity's stare. "In the meantime, I think it couldn't hurt to get to know other artists here too."

Clarity took another bite from the pecan pie as Mariah chimed in again, "Yeah, and while you at it, find out if the brotha who just performed got a girl!"

Both Clarity and Jade turned around to look at Mariah and seeing the other woman stick her neck out with a hand on her hip in complete seriousness, they both laughed.

***

"I knew I shouldn't have let y'all pick out an outfit for me."

Jade looked down at the burnt orange halter top dress and corkscrew wedged shoes she had on and let out a deep sigh. Her friends Xavier and Raquel both circled around her, squealing and smoothing out the imaginary wrinkles on the dress.

"I gotta admit, you were right about the color Raquel. She is poppin' in her lip gloss and glowin' in that orange!" Xavier said with a smile.

Jade watched as Raquel and Xavier high fived one another and rolled her eyes.

"Thank you. And you did the damn thing with her hair! And even though I wish she'd tried a pair of heels, them wedges are cute."

Glaring at the shoes on her feet, Jade puckered her lips in annoyance.

I guess I should be glad that they gave me shoes I can walk in...

Jade snuck a peek over Raquel's head at herself and silently admired her braids that were now in two big buns. Xavier carefully selected a few to leave out, softly sweeping the back of Jade's neck and front of her face.

"So, what do you think?"

Hearing Xavier's voice, Jade stepped forward when Raquel moved to the side toward the long length mirror. She took in the whole look and couldn't stop the smile that made its way to her face.

"Hey Mikey - I think she likes it!" Raquel said smugly.

Xavier cut his eyes at Raquel before adding, "I don't know who no Mikey is, but he ain't getting credit for this look. Cause we did that!"

A knock at the door interrupted their celebration and Jade used it as a way to practice walking more in the unfamiliar shoes. With Xavier and Raquel hot on her heels, Jade wobbled to the front door and turned the knob. When she did, Nashone stared at her and Jade saw his mouth fall open slightly before closing it again.

"Yeah, we did *that*!" Raquel whispered behind Jade, causing Xavier to snort.

Jade kept her eyes on Nashone when she finally found the words to speak, "Hey."

"Hey." Nashone said, sweeping over Jade's look before looking her in the eyes again. "You ready?"

When Jade nodded, she turned to look at her friends, "Thanks y'all for helping me."

"You welcome! Now go and stunt on 'em!" Raquel said.

Nashone reached out a hand and Jade extended hers, but just as quickly stopped. *I can't believe I almost left without Luxe!*

Turning to look at Xavier, Jade started to walk back to her room. "Wait! I need Luxe."

"Jade, the sound stage has other guitars you can use." Nashone stated before adding, "We don't want to be late."

She scrunched up her face at Nashone. "That's cool, but I wanna play with my guitar. Xavier-"

"On it chicka."

Her friend sprinted back down the hallway into her room, and Jade's heart slowed down once she saw Xavier carrying the hardcase she'd put Luxe in earlier that morning. "Thank you."

"You welcome. Now go!" Xavier said, kissing Jade on the cheek.***

The car ride was quiet, and Jade's nervousness appreciated every second of it while Nashone drove her to Guerilla Records. They soon arrived at the three story building, she was shocked at how much it looked like a typical business office. The ground floor exterior seemed to be all glass, allowing anyone passing by to see inside to see the framed records and a few meeting spaces in place. So caught up in taking it all in, Jade didn't realize that Nashone was out of the car until she heard him open the passenger side door.

"Not what you thought, uh?" he asked.

Jade slowly shook her head. "Nah, not at all."

The two chuckled while she took off her seatbelt and stepped out.

"Yeah, me either. But wait until you see the inside." Nashone told her.

Holding the handle of her hard case she let Nashone lead her through the double doors and Jade froze when she saw the security guards that waited passed the front entrance.

Nashone took her hand into his and whispered, "It's just a precaution, since a lot of the artists here have... "

He let the sentence fall off while he strolled toward the metal detectors and beefy men in all black. Once they were close enough, Nashone went first and Jade watched as one of the men waved a black banton looking object around his body. A beeping sound went off and Nashone grinned as he reached into his pockets and took out his car keys. The guard waved the black banton over him again before signaling with his free hand for Nashone to go forward.

Now on the other side, Nashone turned to Jade and sent a soft smile her way when another guard approached her.

"Gear on the converter belt." He gruffly commanded, sharply tilting his head to the opposite side.

When Jade saw the items moving onto the belt and disappearing into a large metal box, she gripped her hard case closer to her side. "I'll get my guitar back, right?" Jade asked before adding quickly, "Once I get on the other side?"

She watched the guard nod once and Jade went over to the beginning of the converter belt. Sighing, she looked at Luxe's case and gently lifted it onto the machine. While her guitar went through the machine, Jade went back to the guard and stood still for inspection, her eyes on the converter belt the entire time. Once she was cleared, she put an extra bounce in her step when she reached the end. Seeing the case come down the belt, Jade grabbed it with both hands."

Let's get you set up in the soundroom." Nashone said.

He continued to lead her down the large path, and Jade could've sworn she heard laughter behind them as they left. But before she could turn around to check, she was faced with a long wall full of more records and pictures.

"Are these the artists of the label?" she asked.

Nashone nodded. "The ones that have gone gold and platinum. A few have since moved on, but Erik likes to keep their accomplishments on the wall. Since they got their start by paying their dues with Guerilla."

They continued down the long hallway until they came to another double door with clear glass. Jade could see the small stage and instruments placed on each end. Her curiosity overrode her nervousness as she reached out and grabbed the golden door hand and yanked it down.

This room still smells new.

Jade strolled over to the stage, passed the rows and rows of theater seats and blinked when another set of warm lights came on around her.

"You think you can make it do what it do in here?"

Turning to Nashone's voice, Jade sat her case onto the table just to the side of the stage. Opening it, she took out Luxe and began placing the multicolor strap to connect to her guitar for later. She took her time, now enjoying the feel of Nashone staring at her. When she turned around, he was sitting in the front row smiling.

"Yeah, I can make it do what it do."

A flight of butterflies fluttered to her chest, settling in around her ribcage. Jade welcomed them with each step she took toward Nashone. By the time she stood in front of him, Jade had turned Luxe around and the two of them locked eyes in the small space.

"I can't wait to hear you do your thing."

Jade knew she was cheesing when her cheeks covered up her eyes, but she didn't care.

"Can I get a kiss? You know, for good luck?"

Nashone started to lean in toward Jade's face but stopped. He looked around the room, "What if - "

She grabbed his face in her hands and brought their lips together. Just like that night, Jade loved the feel of his soft lips against hers. Though before she could re-introduce her tongue to his, Nashone pulled away. With her chest rising and falling after each breath, Jade kept her eyes on Nashone's.

"What happened to you not doing that before?"

Jade felt warm under the low lights when she spoke, "Well, now that I have, I wanna keep doing it."

Nashone's eyes danced over her face, and Jade tried to close the distance and get reacquainted with his lips again. This time Nashone was ready and quickly side stepped her. But when she glanced over at him, the look on Nashone's face made her hopeful. He brought a hand out to touch his lips as he stared at Jade, shaking his head.

"I want to too."

She tried to get closer to him again, but Nashone chuckled when he took two steps back and met her stare. "But first, you gotta get through the showcase. I promise, after that, I won't stop you."

"Okay, whatever." was Jade's reply.

When she brought Luxe around to her chest again, Nashone walked over and grinned.

"Thank you."

Jade rolled her eyes while she strummed absently on her guitar. Until she heard Nashone humming along to the notes. Curious, she looked over and watched as Nashone swayed from side to side.

I wonder if he still knows the words.

While Nashone continued humming, Jade played the intro to the song they were going to perform together during their senior recital. Just as she looked up, Nashone was standing closer than before and Jade almost stopped breathing at the sight of him grinning over at her. She went into strumming the chord progressions gradually, giving him time to come in with the lyrics.

"Springtime at night, all around with you..."

Hearing Nashone sing the first verse to the song, Jade wanted to kiss him all over again. But she focused on the chords and his voice, which sounded deeper than before. Jade hadn't performed with anyone since then, and she was glad that was the case. Though just as they were about to get to the last chorus, the door swung open and Nashone stopped singing. Jade was almost too afraid to, but she willed herself to look at Nashone. Gone was the smile she was getting used to again, and in its place was a stoic stare that Jade couldn't read.

"Was that you playa?"

The guy that marched toward Nashone couldn't have been an artist for Guerilla Records, with his towering height and husky frame. When his baritone voice ranged out, she felt each rumble down her spine.

"We ain't known you could sing homie!"

More people entered the showcase room, their various voices clashing with the atmosphere that Jade had with Nashone minutes ago. She watched as Nashone, the intern for Guerilla Records, came into full view while talking to the small group of people now in the room.

"We all can't be rappers like y'all. " he said with a smile, as laughter followed. When Nashone faced Jade again, she forced herself to smile as he continued.

"Anyways, y'all meet Jade. Erik and the board are thinking about bringing her in to work with a few of you. To help get y'all on the wall with the other greats and shit."

A few girls stepped forward and looked Jade up and down before she recognized one of them. Blaze snickered as she leaned over and whispered into another girl's ear. And Jade felt her hands hold Luxe tight when both girls laughed.

"Is that true?"

Jade looked at the girl now in front of her, who was dressed in a pair of cut-off jean shorts and a jersey that was tied in the back, showing off her pierced belly button. When the smaller girl smiled, Jade returned it as she answered. "I-I hope so."

"That's what's up! But I gotta tell you, I don't know shit about playing that thing, so I'mma leave that all up to you. Call me Super P."

"Super P?"

The girl nodded excitedly, "That's right! Cause you can't say the full name on the radio, I'm trying to get used to not saying it all the time. But, whatever gets me them record sales, right?"

Jade swallowed before nodding and the girl strolled up to Nashone. "She cute."

Nashone looked between them before slowly tilting his head at Jade. "Fo sho."

The double doors opened again, and everyone inside the room grew silent. But when Jade looked back at Nashone, she noticed the way his lips pressed together while his hardened stare followed the people that made their way to the front row."Glad y'all ain't on no CP time, newbie." Erik said to Nashone before acknowledging Jade with a head nod and sitting down. "Let's get this over with, I got an after party to get to."

A few of the guys from earlier chuckled while everyone sat down around him. Everyone except Nashone, who walked over to the side of the wall and stood. Once they all sat, the room was quiet, just like when Jade first walked in. She could hear the live mic and speakers, but avoided walking up the stage to use them.

I barely made it this far with falling on my face in these shoes! Let me not tempt fate.

Instead, Jade walked to the middle of the room, in front of the stage and cleared her throat. "H-hey y'all. For those that don't know, my name's Jade. And I'll be playing for y'all for a bit. Is that alright?"

Silence greeted her and Jade closed her eyes as her fingers got in position for the first song she planned.

"So you wanna be an artist at Guerilla? Playing a guitar?"

Jade looked out into the small crowd and tried to ignore the disdain she heard in the girl's voice. Finding a small glass window near the double doors to focus on, Jade spoke again.

"Well, no. Not an artist. More like...a collaborative songwriter."

"How you see that working? Our female rappers don't get down with a banjo in the studio."

Laughter broke out and Jade closed her eyes before opening them again and prayed her face didn't show how she felt at having to answer their question.

"I'm a trained musician and songwriter. So, I can write and arrange music about anything and tailor it to the person I'm writing for. Does that make sense?"

"Oh. Well, why you ain't just say you was a band geek?"

More laughter rang out, and Jade noticed Nashone start to walk to the front of the room. She looked over at him and slightly shook her head.

Please, please don't do nothin'! You just gonna make it worse.

"I didn't say I was a band geek, cause that's not how I see myself. Just like you wouldn't say you one felony away from going gold."

When one of the guys from earlier jumped out of his seat, Jade rushed out. "It's just bad business, no matter how close to the truth it is."

Jade watched as Erik stood up, smoothing out the front of his three piece suit. "Y'all got anymore questions? Save 'em for later."

He took out his phone before sitting again.

With the room silent, Jade went into her first song, the cover everyone at Clarity's loved. She kept her voice low and controlled until the end, adding an extra run so she could harmonize it with the last chord she played. Once the music faded, she was met with silence again.

Damn. Nothing?

She almost laughed at the ridiculousness of it all, until she remembered that she had two more songs to do for this set.

Whatever. Just sit there and be mad then.

The last two songs were originals, but to show that she had listened to some of the artist's tracks that made it to the radio, Jade switched up the chord progressions and tempo to each, giving them a more dirty south club anthem feel. By the time she finished the last song, Jade could hear a few claps in time to the beat along with more whispers. She turned Luxe around to her side and addressed the crowd again.

"Any questions, comments, requests?"

That line usually got her a few laughs at Clarity's, but here it found nothing but radio silence. Keeping her face neutral, Jade looked over to where Nashone was and saw that he wasn't there.

Where did he go?

"Well, thanks for listening. Enjoy y'all night."

Everyone started to get up to leave, a few took out their phones and snapped her picture. As she started to walk over to her hard case to put Luxe away, Super P skipped over to her with her phone out.

"I texted my cousin about you during your set. Why you ain't say you from Clarity's?"

Jade was surprised, and it must have shown as Super P explained, "Yeah, I got a few peeps that hang out there to listen to new artists and shit. They say you a regular."

"Yeah, I am. Been working there for a few months now."

Super P snapped her fingers excitedly. "That's what's up! Let me get a pic with you right quick."

This time when Jade smiled, it was genuine. "Okay."

"Hey! One of y'all take our pic!"

One of the linebackers looked over at her and Super P pointed, "You! Getcho ole goon squad ass over here and take our picture!"

Jade looked at Super P and the question fell out of her mouth before she could stop herself. "They let you talk shit like that?"

"Oh, so you can cuss! I was wondering for a hot minute when they was trying you before you started performing..."

Jade finally released the laughter she had been holding back since the first song. Soon Super P had joined in, and the two looked at one another and burst into another round of laughs while the guy in front of them held out Super P's phone. Wiping at her eyes, Super P closed the distance between them and grabbed Jade's waist. "You ready?"

Turning to face the guy with Super P's camera, she smiled. "Yeah."

The two posed as they waited to hear the click sound. When the guy gave Super P back her phone, Jade noticed how quiet it was again in the room. She looked around and didn't see Nashone anywhere.

"Hope to see you again."

Jade glanced over at Super P and grinned.

"You too. Have a good night."

She watched as Super P left the room and released a sigh.

Do I really wanna work with these peeps everyday?

As Jade started to remove her strap, she noticed that the top string on her guitar seemed to snag on the fret boards.

I knew it sounded off after the last song. Let me gone and tighten it up again.

Walking over to the small table, Jade sat her guitar down inside the hardcase and started to inspect the string. It had been a minute since she changed this one, so Jade rummaged inside the case for the spare steel strings she kept in the compartment. Opening the small package, she took out the strings and laid them onto the table.

Okay, by the time I finish this, Nashone should be back.

While removing the snagging string from Luxe, Jade heard the double doors open and smiled, expecting Nashone. Her smile fell when she saw that it was Erik instead.

"Is that any way to show your employer love, shawty?" he said.

Jade's brain started working over time as his words sunk in.

He said employer? Does that mean...

"I was - wait, are you saying I got the position?" Jade asked excitedly.

She watched as he unbuttoned the jacket to his suit, along with the cuff links, "Yeah, you got the job."

When he reached the table next to her, Jade smiled again.

"Oh, wow! Um, thank you? Yeah, thank you for the opportunity to work with y'all."

Erik's laugh was low as he stared down at Jade. "Don't thank me yet, shawty, we ain't even get to them positions you talked about."

Jade scrunched her nose up at his word choice before dismissing them. She went to put her guitar back in the hardcase, and as she turned around, Erik quickly went to her side and she could feel all of him against her backside. When she gasped, Jade smelled the alcohol coming off of him and tried to move away.

"Like I said, thank you again. I'm going to go wait for Nashone-"

"Did I say you can leave? Besides, that errand boy is busy." Erik slurred out.

Panic inched its way to Jade's chest, as Erik's hands went to her ass, grabbing it roughly.

"I ain't see all this when you performed at that little coffee shop...See why ya boy wanna get down now."

She pushed her way out of his grasp, and tried to keep her voice low, "D-don't touch me."

"What you say bitch?!" Erik shouted.

Before Jade could get further away, Erik's hand was mid-air and across her face. Jade screamed as the force of his slap sent her facing the table. He then pushed himself against her again, this time rubbing the front of himself on her ass.

"Yeah, let's see what positions you ready for now."

Her whole body went still as his intentions became clear.

No. No!

Jade tried again to get out from under his grip, but Erik pulled on one of her buns and forced her head down to the front of the table.

"That's right, stay right there... Let me break ya big ass in, just like the others."

Tears filled Jade's eyes when she heard the buckle to his belt come undone. His words stuck in her head, and with each re-play, Jade found herself latching onto one word. A word that filled her rage as the tears fell down her cheeks.

By giving in to pressures that weigh them down – That's how gems break.

With granny Gladys' words in her head, Jade thought fast. She spotted the steel strings from earlier still on the table and without hesitation, she grabbed them and curled each one into her hand.

Shouting to the heavens and swinging wildly, Jade whipped the strings over her shoulder.

"The hell?"

When Erik stepped backwards, Jade's whole body trembled as she held onto the steel string and raised her hand.

"No!"

Bringing her hand down swiftly, Jade watched as Erik, with his pants down to his ankles, yell in pain and crouched low, tripping over his own feet. With his hands now in front of his face, Jade moved quickly. Picking up her case, she clutched Luxe to her chest and sprinted to the door. Halfway there, she stumbled as she heard Erik shout from behind.

"You bitch!"

She pushed the double doors open and ran as fast as she could away from the showcase room. Jade kept going, ignoring the blurry faces as she focused on getting out of Guerilla Records. With her chest on fire, Jade bit back a sob when she made it to the exit, trembling as she opened the door.

It was darker outside than before, but Jade remembered she had her Nokia in the compartment of her guitar case. Taking out her phone, she started to enter the number to Clarity's, until she saw the bright lights of a city bus coming her way. Tears stung her eyes as Jade ran again to the large bus stop sign. Luck was on her side, as the bus stopped and she saw someone exiting in the back.

"Wait! Please! Wait!" she shouted.

The driver looked on as Jade reached deep into her compartment case for the fare. She pulled out the only bill she had, which was more than needed, but Jade fed it to the machine anyway. Soon the bus lurched forward, and she almost lost her balance before sitting down. Jade continued to ignore the stares of the other passengers and kept her eyes forward as the bus took her further and further away.

***

Jade didn't know what time it was when she transferred to the bus that got her home. And she didn't care. The house was empty when she stepped inside, and Jade had never been more thankful to be alone in her whole life. Stripping out of the dress that she wore, Jade padded quietly to the kitchen and threw it in the trash, along with the now scuffed up shoes.

She welcomed the chill that greeted her half naked body while going to her room to get her sleeping clothes. Now on autopilot, Jade went to the bathroom and turned on the shower.

I need it hotter.

While turning the water temperature to as hot as she could stand, Jade heard the sound of the front door opening, and her whole body froze. Footsteps quickly made their way down the hallway and Jade held her breath. She winced from each bang that shook the door.

"Jade! Girl, how was the showcase? I wanna hear everything!"

The sound of Xavier's cheerful voice reached her ears and Jade slowly started to relax under the hot water.

I'm home, safe.

With the adrenaline gone and the weight of everything that went down not too long ago starting to crash down around her, Jade broke out into a sob. A sob that left her crying hard, even when she squatted low and under the shower head, letting the water soothe her from head to toe.

"Jade? What's wrong chicka?" The knocks at the door become more insistent, as Jade refused to answer. "What happened, Jade? Are you okay?"

No. I'm not okay.

As the water ran cold, Jade stayed on the floor for what felt like forever before finding the strength to pull herself up and turning it off. Putting on fresh clothes, she went to open the bathroom door, and when she slowly opened it, Jade saw Xavier and Clarity waiting.

"Thank you for calling me. I'll stay with her."

Seeing Clarity there waiting for her, Jade didn't have strength left to fight the new tears that fell as she crumbled into Clarity's embrace. The small circles that Clarity rubbed onto Jade's back had her fading in and out of consciousness. Slowly, the older woman pulled away, looking down at Jade in her arms. And without a word, she led Jade to her room and helped her get into bed before walking out of her room and closing the door.

Chapter Twelve
A New Day

A week passed before Jade could say a word to anyone.

She watched from the window in her room as the sun rose and set. In between those moments, Jade waited to hear Xavier leave for work before coming out and walking around the living room. Flashes of getting ready for that night, seeing Nashone entered Jade's mind and she scurried back to her room, making sure the door was locked before getting back under the covers. Until one day, or night - she'd stopped checking her phone and didn't bother with putting it on the charger - Jade padded into the living room and saw what looked like dust on the flat screen TV.

I have to get it clean.

Springing into action, Jade marched into the kitchen and took out a pair of plastic gloves, along with a duster, cleaning spray, and a roll of paper towels. Soon she was in front of the TV, wiping it down completely, down to the cords that were behind the entertainment stand. Still not satisfied, Jade dragged the stand away from the wall and found more dust and dirt to get rid of. Going back to the kitchen, she brought out the broom and dustpan to sweep up the mess.

It's all still dirty. I have to clean!

While Jade looked around the living room, she wasted no time pushing the couches away from the walls, pulling up the rugs and moving the table and end table. Before she knew it, Jade had cleaned the entire living room. But everything looked out of place. Exhausted, she trodded to the bathroom to take a shower. When Jade started to remove her clothes, she turned away and caught a glimpse of her reflection in the mirror. The thought that immediately followed the sight sent her to the floor.

I'm still dirty.

Erik's voice still rang in her head, and Jade wanted to make it go away. Taking deep breaths, she pulled herself upward and looked anywhere but the mirror when she turned on the shower. The warm water felt like a balm as it rolled down her skin. Jade took her time scrubbing herself, slowly inhaling and exhaling while watching the bubbles before rinsing them away. Turning off the water, Jade got dressed and headed back to her room.

When she left the bathroom, Jade saw Xavier waiting by her bedroom door. She noticed he was barefoot but still wearing his work polo shirt and slacks. Xavier was mid-turn and came to a stop when he saw her. She immediately went to look away, but Xavier's soft tone got Jade to look him in the eye.

"I don't know what happened and you don't have to tell me."

Jade watched as Xavier wrung his hands together before shoving them into the pockets of his slacks. "But Jade - you give me a name. Cause my abuela taught me some shit before she passed away, and I swear - you give me a name and I'll get whoever hurt you."

Jade went to take a step forward, but paused as she blinked back tears. She watched Xavier as he stayed in front of her room door and he kept his hands inside the pockets of his slacks. As she started walking toward him again, Jade saw a small smile grace Xavier's face just before she threw her arms around his neck.

"Thanks."

One of Xavier's hands patted the top of Jade's head and she brought her shoulders inward before he moved his hand away. When he did, Jade broke the hug and looked down at the carpet.

"For helping me, even before... and for calling Clarity. Just for everything, Xavier. Thanks."

Jade looked at Xavier again and saw the unshed tears in his eyes as he nodded quickly. When he stepped to the side of her door, Jade went back into her room and pressed her head against the door, turning the lock.

Looking at her bed, Jade made her way to it until the sight of her hard case caught her eye. She hadn't played Luxe since that night. Now, as she looked at the case, her hands itched. Curling her left hand, Jade took her time walking over to the case as she knelt down. It was dinged up pretty bad at the bottom, and one of the latches had started to fall off. Reaching out a hand, Jade snatched it back and away from the case.

I need to see it. I want to see Luxe.

After a few deep breaths, Jade tried again to open the case. The creaking sound when opening it almost hurt her ears, but once she saw Luxe inside, Jade felt her heart rate pick up. She lightly touched the wooden body and bridge while looking up at the tuning head and frets. Taking it out of the case, Jade placed her fingers along the first few frets and froze. For the first time since getting Luxe on her birthday, Jade didn't know what to do. Her fingers wobbled over the frets, clanked against the pegs, and she found herself hunched over while holding the guitar, looking at each string as though she forgot how they made sound.

Wh-what's wrong? Why I'm bugging right now?

Jade's chest tightened as she tried to focus on remembering the different notes and chords. After a few minutes of struggling, she dropped her left hand and pushed Luxe away. This time, tears of frustration welled up in Jade's eyes when she looked back at her guitar.

Why? Why can't I play?

Wiping her face with the back of her hand, Jade sat up and looked for her phone.

Her work study ended days before going to Guerrilla, but she wasn't worried about that gig.

Might as well see if I still have a job at the coffee shop.

But when the words crossed her mind, Jade's whole body went rigid. The thought of being surrounded by all those customers and noises that came with being at Clarity's left Jade clutching her chest.

What is wrong with me? I have to work!

Thinking of work, Jade tried to remember where she last saw her phone. The day after being at Guerilla Records, she got sick of hearing it ring, so Jade tossed it inside her closet. She sighed as she made her way to the closet and scanned the floor. Sure enough, the Nokia was in between a pair of old sneakers. Jade squatted down and picked up the phone, taking it to the nightstand and plugging it into the charger.

Jade knew it would take time until she'd be able to call Clarity's, so to keep herself busy, she sat down next to Luxe. The more she glanced down at her guitar, the further away Erik's words got in her mind. Soon, the only words Jade heard were granny Gladys', and she picked up Luxe again. Holding the guitar, Jade took another deep breath and let it out in a rush while putting the guitar back into the hardcase.

***

The next day, she'd woken up sore from falling asleep on the floor next to Luxe. Taking her time, she got up off the floor and noticed that her phone had a full charge. It was still early, and she knew it was a risk to go to Clarity's without calling, but she had to try.

It'd been a minute since Jade had put on jeans, much less gone outside. The denim pants felt restricting against her legs, and Jade knew she'd work up a sweat waiting for the bus, but she slipped them on anyway. Along with a light long sleeve shirt, she grabbed her hard case and messenger bag before walking to the front door. With her hand now in front of the door handle, Jade paused.

I can do this. I need to do this.

Her right hand felt like a lead as she touched the door knob. Turning it, Jade stepped back and let the sun spill into the opening space. She stared down at the contrast of light on her black sneakers and tried moving one foot in front of the other. But it wouldn't move. Her heart raced the more Jade stood still, until her left hand started to ache. One small step turned into two, and before long, Jade found herself looking up and squinting at the sun.

The bus stop bench was empty, which she'd hoped for. Though by the time she got to it and sat Luxe down, Jade could see the bus zipping toward her.

Picking back up the case, Jade closed her eyes and listened as the bus roared closer to the stop. Soon the bus screeched in front of Jade, and she felt the cool air condition from inside blast into her face. Stepping inside and swiping her monthly pass, Jade was thankful to see that there weren't too many people inside as the bus lurched forward. Once she propped Luxe up beside her in the middle of the buses' standing area, Jade dug inside her bag and took out her headphones. Pressing play onto the CD player inside, she listened to the rhythmic sounds as the bus moved on.

Her bus ride was quick, with fewer people getting on and off during the transit. Before Jade knew it, she was two stops away from Clarity's. Quickly shutting off the CD player and putting away her headphones, Jade waited until the bus passed the next stop and pressed the stop request button. Getting off the bus, Jade looked out at the coffee shop and for the first time in days felt lighter. She breathed in the air around her and almost sprinted to the front door.

When she reached it, Jade saw Joe moving the speakers from out of the instrument room and turned the handle. Quietly she entered the coffee shop and the soft sounds of Classic R&B floated around in the space, bouncing off of the wall to Jade's ears. She took in the sounds and slowly looked around, seeing that everything was the same.

"Jade!"

Joe's booming voice interrupted her thoughts, and Jade watched as the older man moved fast toward her. "Baby girl..."

Hearing his voice made Jade's heart smile. But when Joe reached out to hug her, Jade tightly shut her eyes and froze into place.

"I-I'm sorry. My Clarity told me not-"

Jade shook her head. "It's okay. I'm okay."

Joe stood in front of her, and Jade cautiously closed the distance between them. When she felt Joe's strong arms wrap around hers, Jade willed herself not to cry. She brought her hands out around Joe's back and he hugged her tighter before letting go.

"Clarity said - she said you might need some time off."

Hearing the gravel sound of Joe's voice, Jade looked up and saw him wiping at his face with a handkerchief. She waited until Joe looked at her again before asking, "Do I still have my job? I-I wanna start working again."

Joe looked at her for so long without speaking that Jade was afraid to hear his answer. She quickly offered, "I can even work overtime if you need me to."

"You ain't got to do that. Your job still here, baby girl."

Jade heard the crack in Joe's voice as he spoke, and she started to say thank you. But with a wave of his handkerchief, Joe silenced her.

"Don't feel rushed to come back here, Jade. We'll be here when you's ready."

She nodded and Joe cleared his throat before continuing, "You can stay and wait for Clarity to come back from the market up the road, but that's it. See her and gone on home."

After spending days in the house, Jade immediately shook her head at the thought of doing that again. She looked down at her case and whispered one last request. "Can I play here for a little while? At least until Clarity comes back?"

Joe dabbed at the corner of his eyes before answering. "Sure. Play as long as you want."

Walking to the stage, Jade bent down to take her guitar out of the case. With Luxe in her hands, Jade went to the nearest stool and sat down, her eyes looking up at the tealights. They weren't turned on yet, but the natural light that passed through from the large windows reflected off of them, causing them to gleam. Jade placed her left hand on the neck of her guitar, letting her fingers guide her into the first chord she learned. The sound of the C major chord ranged out and Jade lips turned upward.

I didn't forget. I...I just needed reminding.

Memories of her granny and playing the guitar for her on Sunday afternoons flashed in and out of Jade's mind. She kept strumming the rest of the chords from muscle memory and sighed when she started to recall the more complex ones she learned over the years. Her pace picked up as she plucked some notes, but when she played the B flat minor - the last chord Jade remembered playing at Guerilla Records - she stopped.

Jade's right hand shook as she quickly changed into second position onto the guitar. Her mouth partly opened, but she didn't dare speak while letting the events from that night replay in her mind. As more tears threatened to leave her eyes, Jade whipped her head back and forth.

I'm so sick of crying!

Dropping her head down toward Luxe, Jade didn't fight the heat that spread across her face. When it made its way down to her neck, she gripped Luxe and snapped her head back up, pressing down hard on the C minor chord. Her anger came out not only from the hard and fast strumming, but when she opened her mouth again. Jade's scream left her throat as her lungs expanded, giving her the space and air she needed.

With her chest rising and falling, Jade muted Luxe with her right hand, enjoying the vibrations that she felt. When the vibes stopped, she reached out her hand and strummed the D chord, and fast as lightning, Jade slapped down on Luxe again. She kept at it, switching notes and muting the guitar with her hands. Plucking fast at each string, Jade ignored the pain in her fingers until she couldn't anymore.

Letting go of the last string, Jade looked back up at the tealights while the last note rang out. With the house music playing lower than normal, it made the silence that welcomed Jade feel unusual at the coffee shop, which made Jade finally look out around the inside of Clarity's. When she did, Jade wanted to shut her eyes and be anywhere else as she took in the view of not only Joe, but Clarity and Nashone.

Jade looked on as Clarity held out her hands over Joe's chest, trying to keep him from getting closer to Nashone.

"Joe, we don't know what happened. Let's wai-"

For the first time since knowing the two, Jade heard Joe cut Clarity off as he growled, "We know whatever baby girl is going through right now gots to do with him! I bet the house on that!"

Even from the stage, Jade could see Joe's hand shake as he tried to get closer to Nashone.

"You got some nerve showing your face in here boy."

Jade continued to stare as Clarity turned to look back at Nashone.

"He's been calling the coffee shop every day, Joe. So when I came in from the back entrance and saw you talking with Jade, I called him and told him to come."

This is all my fault, I should be the one to end it.

Jade stood, placing Luxe down onto the stool and she could feel all three of them staring at her as she approached. She steadied her breathing before looking at Nashone.

"We need to talk."

Not waiting for him to answer, Jade walked to the nearest table. Clarity took Joe's hand and dragged him to the barista station. She and Nashone sat down at the table and she stared at Nashone. Every day Jade spent at home, she thought about what she wanted to say to him, but now as she watched him, with bags under his eyes and a five o'clock shadow settling in on his face, Jade wasn't sure which question to start with first. That was until she saw him open his mouth.

Jade shook her head before asking, "Why did you leave after the showcase?"

Nashone cut his eyes away for a beat, before meeting her stare.

"I got a message from Jon to go and set up the conference room for another meeting. When I finished and tried to go back to the showcase...security told me you'd... they said you'd left."

Jade swallowed the lump that was forming in her throat.

"Do you know what happened? After...after my set?"

Nashone leaned forward, placing his hands on the table. His eyes were wide as he spoke, "When I heard from security, I had them pull the video. Jade..."

Jade turned her head away when she felt tears stinging her eyes.

"Erik went MIA right after the showcase. And I've been trying to get a hold of you ever since. That's why I'm here Jade. To see if you're—"

"To see if I what? Want to press charges? Will go to the media?"

Nashone hung his head before leveling back to look at her.

"I-I wanted to see you. To make sure you're okay."

"I'm not."

The two stared at one another before Nashone whispered, "I ain't want this to happen."

"But you knew it would though, right? That's why you were buggin' when I talked about meeting with him. And when you asked me not to do the showcase when we were downtown that day..."

Nashone didn't answer, so Jade continued, "You knew he was a monster in a suit, selling hopes and dreams to folks like me. And you still put me in the same room as him. For what? A promotion?"

"It wasn't like that Jade! I swear! I-I thought I could protect you."

The laugh that left Jade's lips was bitter. "I needed you to be my friend and be straight with me about what I was walking into."

Jade looked away and blinked the pain behind her tears away. "Guess not much has changed. You still know how to dip without warning, uh?"

"Jade..."

"Nah, at least now I know for sure. First it was 'cause your parents and now it's 'cause you've gotten used to wearing nice suits."

Nashone started to speak again but Jade stood.

"I wish you well, Nashone. And I'm sure you know not to come here again."

Not waiting to hear him speak, Jade walked back to the stage. She placed Luxe back into the hard cover case and turned around just in time to see Nashone's tear stained face as he walked out of Clarity's.

"You okay baby girl?" Joe asked softly.

Another tear slid down Jade's cheek and she quickly brushed it away before turning to face him and Clarity. "I will be."

June 2003

Epilogue

Three weeks later...

With the morning and last exam done, Jade couldn't wait to leave campus.

The news about Guerilla Records came in earlier that following week and the buzz surrounding Erik Sharpe's run for the border and eventual arrest had spread like wildfire around the otherwise quiet school.

After talking it over with Clarity and Joe, they took her to the police and she filed a report. Though what followed was not what any of them expected. Apparently, the police department had an informant working undercover at the record label as security, and when Jade showed up to report what happened that night, that gave the precinct what they needed to get a search warrant for Guerilla Records.

More victims came forward once the police swarmed the company, and before long they had enough to charge the CEO with assault, battery, and racketeering. Once news got out, Erik had nowhere else to hide, which led him to make an attempt to flee to Mexico.

Just thinking about the cliche madness of it all still made Jade laugh.

I hope he never sees the outside again.

The last she heard while at work was that Jon Morae, the former A&R, now interim CEO, was in talks of buying Erik's former position so he could afford his court fees. Nashone was being trained as his successor, after agreeing to testify against his former boss.

Jade tried to not let her thoughts go to him as she walked to the campus bus stop, but it was no use. Everyone at work had been extra cautious about even saying his name, but they couldn't stop customers from doing the same. And with him all over the news, standing by a few executives and the Guerilla Records legal team, Jade couldn't escape seeing him.

She wasn't sure if he would respect her wishes and stay away at first, but he did that and more.

Weeks after reporting Erik, Jade thought she would have to take the stand when the news came out about the trial. Days went by and she was on edge waiting to be subpoenaed. Instead of being summoned by the law, an attorney strolled into the coffee shop with a certified envelope. After she signed for it and opened the letter, she promptly sat down at seeing the check inside.

The attorney explained that per the deal his client Mr. Daniels negotiated with the opposing prosecutor, she was to be excluded from taking the stand and given the five-figure check for emotional distress suffered while at Guerilla Records. After hearing that, the attorney handed her another letter and left.

She recognized Nashone's handwriting right away and tore the letter open. Reading that while at work wasn't her smartest idea, but it did give her what she needed where her former friend was concerned.

Jade allowed herself to think of him one last time for the day before slipping on her headphones. Though when she took them out of her bag, her phone ranged.

"Heya Clarity! Everything okay?" she asked.

"No, not really." Clarity quickly added, "We've got an unexpected rush - after I sent home the new part timer. Could you come help out?"

Jade tapped her pass on the ticket machine and sat at the first window seat. "I'm on my way."

As the bus came to a stop, Jade looked out the window toward the coffeeshop. There were about half a dozen or so cars out front, not nearly as many as she expected after Clarity's call.

She hopped off the bus and took off her headphones while walking up to the entrance. It was even quieter than usual, with only the sounds of the smooth oldie joints that Joe liked playing in the background.

Though she still made her way to the door, turning the knob before walking in. Seeing no one, Jade tried to keep the worry out of her voice while she stepped further inside and called out, "Clarity! Where is th-"

"SURPRISE!"

Jade slightly jumped, placing her hand over chest.

In front of her was not only Clarity and Joe, but practically everyone she held dear in this world. Xavier and Diamond cheered while her nephew Dimar covered his ears. Even Mariah and Raquel, both wearing Clarity's coffee shop t-shirts, waved streamers while rushing toward her.

"Happy Birthday baby girl!" Joe announced with a smile.

Jade took them all in, as Clarity came from behind the stage.

"All of this is for me?" Jade asked before adding, "But my birthday isn't until next week."

Clarity made her way through some of her classmates and a few artists that Jade had begun to get to know from performing at the weekly open mics.

"I'm sorry for tricking you to come here like this, but as you said, your birthday is next week and we wanted to surprise you."

"That you did." Jade laughed, "But how's this a surprise birthday party without a birthday cake?"

"Oh! We got you sis!" Diamond shouted.

Jade watched as Xavier and Raquel took off behind the counter, bickering the whole way. Her eyes grew as they carefully stepped back out, each holding a large white sheet cake. Complete with a treble clef, notes, and staffs, just like what you'd find on actual sheet music. And in the center was her name with 'happy birthday' scrolled below.

As the two sat the cake on the nearest table, Clarity raised a hand and Jade was treated to the most heartwarmingly ridiculous birthday song she'd ever heard.

***

An hour passed after they all had their fill of cake. Everyone was dancing and cracking jokes while Jade and Diamond took turns swaying on the floor with her nephew on either of their hips.

When the last song ended, Joe made his way over to them, his eyes full of merriment when he held out a hand. "Excuse me y'all, but can I cut in?"

Looking at Diamond with Dimar on her hip, Jade beamed. "Anytime!"

Dimar went to reach out for Jade and Diamond took his hand into hers, "Tee Tee will be back little man. Besides, I need to rest my feet anyway."

Sharing a look with Diamond, Jade's chest swelled as she nodded and turned to face Joe.

He extended his hand and Jade accepted it before and they two stepped their way out onto the makeshift stage. When the song ended, Joe stopped and gestured toward the stage. "Me and the missus got somethin' to show you."

Joe didn't give her a chance to ask before he led her to the stage where Clarity already stood. When they reached the two small steps, Jade saw a guitar box with a huge red bow laying on the floor.

"Well, I ain't see no way to wrap it without you guessin' what it was no way, so ..."

Jade looked on between Joe and Clarity, who leaned in close to Joe and put a hand on his shoulder.

"Now this ain't to replace your first one, we'd never do that. But we wanted to get you something that came from our hearts." Clarity pressed her lips onto his forehead and Joe's voice crackled in the air as he added, "And I know how much Luxe means to ya, but me and the missus wanted you to know how much you come to mean to us."

Jade walked slowly to the stage and picked up the box. Laying it on top of the stool, she removed the top and gasped.

"Is that - is that what I think it is?" Jade asked in excited disbelief. Looking at Joe and Clarity, she reached inside the box and gingerly picked up the guitar.

"And 'fore you say it's too much, 'member, it's a sought after gift." Joe explained.

"It's a 1960, not 1959. That's why it looks almost the same as my Joe's." Clarity offered before adding. "He already got it tuned for you to play."

"Only the best for my baby girl." Joe proudly stated. "Whatcha gonna name it?"

As he and Clarity shared a laugh, Jade pushed the lump down her throat.

"Well, you ain't gotta give it a name now," Joe added, "I just know that's something you like doing, so make sure it's a good one."

Looking up at them, Jade's eyes filled with tears. "Thank you." she whispered. The tears soon began to wet her cheeks as she fought to speak again over the burning knot in her throat. "Thank y'all so much...for e-everything."

Jade thought back on the last few years of her life - the highs and lows, along with all the people she got to know and now hold dear. Her Granny Gladys' words echoed in her head that night after the showcase, but so did Clarity's. And Joe's. And her sister and friends. Jade found herself feeling so many things all at once, every emotion flooded her heart. Weighing it down yet comforting it at the same time until more joyous tears threaten to leave her eyes.

With every hard lesson that came her way, Jade thought for sure that those hits were going to keep her down. But somehow, someway, Jade managed to get up and fight another day - no matter what came her way.

She looked on as they made their way closer. Joe took out an old green bandana and wiped at his face while Clarity kissed Jade's cheeks, before looking up to the ceiling and smiling through a fresh set of tears of her own.

"Can I play CJ now? I got an idea for a new song and wanna know what y'all think."

"CJ?" Joe asked, curious.

When Jade looked at the two of them again, Clarity's light laugh ranged out as Joe joined her with a low chuckle. "CJ, uh? Not bad."

Grinning wide enough to split her face, Jade sent Joe a wink. "I thought you might like that. So, can I play it for y'all?"

Clarity gave Jade another hug before letting go. "Sure baby. You got a title in mind for this new song?"

Jade went back to CJ and removed it slowly from the box. Getting her fingers into the C minor position, Jade closed her eyes and softly plucked each string before strumming downward. Hearing the chord rang through loud and clear, Jade turned back to Clarity and Joe with another blinding smile.

Thank You

Please leave a review on your favorite website so that others may decide if *Hits Keep Coming* would be a great story for them to get into.

And thank you for taking a chance on an indie author. I hope you'll continue to do so in the future.

Until next time,

K. McCoy

MAGIX

Hallyu: A Chinese term, which translates to 'the Korean wave', refers to the globally popular South Korean entertainment industry.

Mika Collins, a fresh out of work English teacher in South Korea, has her otherwise quiet life turned upside down at the unexpected arrival of her wildly outspoken yet lovable childhood friend Isabelle McGrant. The two spark the curiosity of a struggling actress after one random night on the town. They join a struggling agency and the two other girls are not interested in being a part of a girl group.

Will the new group rise to stardom, or crash under the Hallyu wave?

Epic Clubbing

(excerpt from MAGIX, book one)

The bassline from inside the club speakers matched Mika's heartbeat and sent her straight into a trance. She found herself looking out into the crowd with excitement as Izzy gripped her wrist and let out a small yelp. "This is going to be the best night ever!" Izzy squealed. Mika looked over to Geegi, who also was wearing a big smile on her face. Mika gave her new partner-in-crime for the night a light nudge. The two then shared a laugh as Izzy went bouncing back and forth between them. The popular club, ShineON, was not yet crowded with flirtatious bodies, so they could still talk without having to shout over the music.

"How did your friend know about this place?" Geegi asked Mika.

Mika shook her head.

"I honestly do not know. This place must have been tagged by a K-pop group."

Izzy then broke away from them and went twirling around them in a circle, gaining the attention of several other club dancers.

"This place is... Jjang!"

A few guys cheered and raised their drinks in the air after hearing Izzy's outburst.

"Is she always this full of energy?" Geegi asked.

"Yes!" Mika shouted as she took Izzy's hand and spun her around. "And it can be so contagious!" she finished before taking Izzy by the waist with her other hand and sending her into a small dip.

* * *

Mika watched from the corner of her eye as Geegi looked at the two, and chuckled lightly when Izzy took out her phone to record their dancing.

In the mood to live it up and give their new friend a show, Mika and Izzy wasted no time falling into step with the new song that blared through the speakers. It had been so long since she let herself truly enjoy the moment like this, and not wanting to rush it, Mika started off with a few two-steps as Izzy leaned into her.

Izzy flashed a wicked grin when the beat dropped and Mika knew it was her cue to crank it up. They both jumped in unison and threw their hands into the air. Geegi cheered while waving her phone and Mika laughed as Izzy blew a kiss to the growing crowd. Not to be outdone just yet, Mika strutted halfway to Izzy and stopped before bending and dipping her upper body to the floor and slowly winding her hips as she brought herself back up.

Seeing Geegi's mouth opened a bit as she watched them through her phone caused Mika to bite the corner of her bottom lip.

"Get it unnie!" Izzy cheered.

A small crowd formed around them and Izzy mimicked the moves that Mika had done just seconds ago, before adding a more direct come-here motion with her hands. She then crossed her arms over her chest and swayed around before shaking her hair to and fro and jumping from side to side. Mika then slid even closer to her and took her hands again, leading them into a series of twists and turns, making Izzy cackle out loud.

The pair then let go of each other, and Izzy walked provocatively around Mika, who sent her hips into a figure-eight motion as she vogued in front of Izzy. Once Izzy stopped walking around her, Mika did the same.

"Is that all you got, Youngi-ya?" Mika teased.

When Izzy narrowed her eyes, Mika took two steps back. She knew Izzy was about to bring out something wild to the floor and sure enough, Izzy did. A second after the beat changed and sped up in double time, Izzy repeatedly lifted her feet one at a time as she shook her hands and moved her chest in time with the music. Mika let out a laugh as she stopped in front of Izzy, who was now grinning widely.

"I can not believe you remember that move. Haven't done that in years!" Mika said with a smile before clapping slowly.

Izzy jumped into her arms. "Meekeeahh! I have missed you!"

The two hugged one another and swayed side to side before they turned to see Geegi staring at them. They then looked at each other and back to Geegi as they reached out their hands and brought her in between them.

"How did you even find this club, Izzy?" Mika asked over the growingly loud music.

Izzy answered while swaying, her head tilted up to the ceiling as bright neon lights flashed across her face, "Oh! Sandee from SmoothE posted about it on her SNS last weekend."

Mika chuckled as she turned to face Geegi. "Told you so!"

The three of them continued dancing with Geegi in the middle and Mika wanted to stay in that moment forever.

This is the best night in Seoul ever!

Find out what happens next by getting your own copy of **MAGIX** today!
Available via e-book at most major retailers.

Detailed Trigger Warning

Assault scene in chapter eleven and mentions of assault in chapters eleven, twelve, and epilogue.

—

Don't miss out!

Visit the website below and you can sign up to receive emails whenever K. McCoy publishes a new book. There's no charge and no obligation.

https://books2read.com/r/B-A-VWLI-NDSOG

BOOKS 2 READ

Connecting independent readers to independent writers.

Did you love *Hits Keep Coming*? Then you should read *The New E.R.A.*[1] by K. McCoy!

The United States government lied - again.

They convinced desperate citizens, looking to escape the next monstrous wave of the never ending epidemic into signing up as part of a nation wide experiment that, if successful, would make their immune systems invincible to further viruses.

Of the half a million Americans believed to have taken the vaccine, only thousands survived.

But of those that have survived they were, in fact, reborn.

With a thirst for vengeance and blood.

Read more at https://authorkmccoy.com.

Also by K. McCoy

MAGIX
MAGIX
MAGIX: Melodic Whirlwinds

Standalone
A Dove's Cry
A Season to Love
Cupid's Kiss
Holiday Bliss
Doves Cry Too
The New E.R.A.
Hits Keep Coming

Watch for more at https://authorkmccoy.com.

About the Author

K. McCoy is an independent author who enjoys writing across several genres. In her many years of self-publishing, she has traveled around the world, crafting stories based on real-world experiences, combined with hopeful possibilities. Using the knowledge gained within her authorship, K. McCoy now speaks to others virtually and in-person on a variety of subjects within the author community. And through those workshops, she helps authors write drama filled, heart gripping, and authentic stories. As a serial hobbyist, you can find K. McCoy studying other languages, tinkering with an old camera, or trying out a new Yoga pose when she's not writing or working on another bittersweet yet somehow still loveable story. You can find out how to connect with K.McCoy by visiting her on all socials under authorkmccoy.

Read more at https://authorkmccoy.wordpress.com/.

Empowering dreams. Inspiring success.

About the Publisher

be a muse productions, LLC Established in 2024

A creative publishing company that looks to uplift independent authors and promote their stories to diverse readers.

Read more at https://beamuseproductions.wordpress.com/.

www.ingramcontent.com/pod-product-compliance
Lightning Source LLC
Chambersburg PA
CBHW051822170626
46807CB00003B/980